IT TAKES A MIRACLE

JAMEY MOODY

It Takes A Miracle

Edited: Kat Jackson

Cover: Lucy Bexley

Thank you for purchasing my book! I hope you enjoy the story. If you'd like to stay updated on future releases, you can visit my website or sign up for my mailing list here.

www.jameymoodyauthor.com

As an independent author, reviews are greatly appreciated.

I'd love to hear from you!

email: jameymoodyauthor@gmail.com

 Created with Vellum

ALSO BY JAMEY MOODY

Live This Love

The Your Way Series:

Finding Home

Finding Family

Finding Forever – early 2021

To My Parents

I know you always thought you were doing what was best for me and ultimately all you wanted was for me to be happy.

PROLOGUE

"Is anything better than walking hand in hand with your girl, admiring all the twinkling lights and Christmas decorations?" Vanessa mused while bumping her shoulder against Makenna's. She would remember this night for the rest of her life. The smell of holiday wassail drifting from the storefront doors combined with Christmas carols piped through speakers around the town square made the atmosphere festive.

Makenna squeezed her hand. "Your girl? I like the sound of that."

Vanessa pulled her behind a tree and wrapped her arms around a gasping Makenna. She looked into those dark mahogany eyes and lost her breath. Their lips came together as they had so many times before. Makenna had soft full lips that she could kiss forever. When their tongues met a spark shot through Vanessa and a moan hummed deep in her throat.

"You'll always be my girl," Vanessa said breathlessly, pressing her forehead to Makenna's.

"As much as I'm enjoying this stroll, are you ready to go? These kisses are like Christmas gifts and I want to open every one." With a gentle tug, Makenna led Vanessa away. They walked hand in hand and quickly got into Makenna's car.

"I'm so happy your grandparents are letting you spend the night with me," she said, starting the engine.

"I know. Sorry I'm so paranoid about my parents finding out about us that I made you drive to another town. There's no way anyone we know would be here and I loved walking hand in hand with you tonight."

"I loved it too but your parents aren't supposed to be back until the day after tomorrow. We still have two days and lots of time to hold hands," she said, grabbing Vanessa's hand.

"I'm going to be holding more than your hand later tonight." Vanessa leaned over and kissed Makenna on the cheek. "If my parents knew we were together they'd lock me up so fast it wouldn't be funny."

"I think my parents might actually be okay with it."

"Really? What makes you say that?"

"My brother likes to tease me about being gay and he told me that he thinks Mom and Dad would understand."

"Do you think they're wondering why you haven't dated anyone since summer?"

"I told them that I fell in love with the Perry's granddaughter and only have eyes for her."

Vanessa swatted Makenna's arm. "Very funny." She caressed Makenna's hand and pressed her lips to the back of it. "Kenna, everyone may call us kids and in some ways we still are, but I know in my heart that I'll always love you. Always."

"Nessa, I'll always love you too and I intend to show you how much tonight."

Vanessa looked at Makenna's profile as she kept her eyes on the road. She imagined them both at college: no parents to worry about, just them. Happily ever after, that's what she saw.

Makenna glanced over and saw the look on her face. "What are you thinking about?"

"The future and how good ours is going to be." Vanessa smiled dreamily. "Hey, don't forget we have to run by my grandparents' and get my bag. I was so excited to get away from prying eyes that I forgot it."

"It's okay. No prying eyes at my house."

"Good because I'm going to love on you all night long."

Makenna steered the car into Vanessa's grandparents' driveway and her headlights revealed another car.

"Oh no! That's my mom's car. What is she doing here?" Vanessa said worriedly. "I'll run in and get my bag. Be right back," she said, kissing the back of Makenna's hand before dropping it.

Makenna had a bad feeling in her stomach. They had been planning for this night since the summer, knowing that Vanessa came to see her grandparents for Christmas. She thought back to the whirlwind that was Vanessa Perry and how she had blown in like a summer storm and changed Makenna's life forever. It was love at first sight, even though neither had kissed a girl before. That didn't seem to matter once their eyes met and a knowing smile formed on each one's face. They had been together every day right up until Vanessa had to leave to go home and pack for college.

Now, Makenna peered out the windshield and could see shadows behind the living room drapes. When Vanessa had left for college, Makenna thought she might hear from her occasionally, but surprisingly, Vanessa did more than that. She called when she could and wrote her the most beautiful love letters. They emailed nearly every day and counted down the days until Vanessa could come visit her grandparents again for Christmas.

The minutes ticked by and Makenna's anxiety grew until she saw Vanessa running toward the car. She let out a breath she hadn't realized she'd been holding. Vanessa ran to her window and Makenna quickly rolled it down.

"Something weird is going on. My parents told me to pack my stuff because we're leaving in the morning." Vanessa's eyes were wide and she was breathing hard.

"What's wrong?"

"I don't know. It feels like I'm in trouble, but they haven't said anything yet. I told them I was spending the night with you, but they said I couldn't." Vanessa looked at the house and back down at Makenna, disappointment shining in her eyes.

Makenna put her hand over Vanessa's on the door frame and looked up into her troubled face.

"I'm sorry, Ken. I told them you were waiting so I ran out the door. My grandmother kept looking at me with these sad eyes."

"I don't want to leave you. Nessa—"

"It'll be okay. I'll call you later when they explain what's going on. I'm really sorry about tonight." Vanessa pulled Makenna's hand between both of hers and looked back at the house again. She leaned down, squeezing Makenna's hand. "I love you, baby. Don't ever forget that." She quickly kissed Makenna's lips then walked back to the house.

Makenna yelled, "Wait!" Vanessa turned around. "I love you too," she said, just loud enough for Vanessa to hear.

Vanessa smiled and waved. Then she turned and was gone.

"Waterfalls" by TLC was playing on the radio when she realized tears were falling down her cheeks. Makenna drove home, feeling worried and sad.

Later that night Makenna's cheery ringtone exploded into the silence of her room.

"Hello," she said hurriedly. "Vanessa?"

Vanessa whispered into the phone. "Makenna, they know. I have to make this quick."

"How do they know?"

"They snooped in my room and found the sweet card you gave me when I got here. They're taking me home tomorrow and threatened to make me live at home and go to school there. I had to promise not to see you or talk to you anymore."

"Vanessa!"

"I'm so sorry. Kenna, I convinced them that I'm not gay, that it's just you, so they're giving me a chance."

"A chance? What do you mean?"

"They said if I don't talk to you or see you that they'll let me go back to the university."

"What do we do now?"

"I'm really scared, Makenna. I'll write to you when I get back to school. Please don't try to call me or write me at home."

"But—"

"They're coming," she whispered. "Remember, I'll always love you, Kenna. Always." The call ended.

Makenna received one letter after Christmas. In it, Vanessa begged her not to write or call because her parents were watching her even while she was away at college. After that, there was nothing but silence.

And just like that the whirlwind that was Vanessa Perry stormed out of Makenna's life, taking her heart with her.

1

Makenna could see her reflection on the computer screen. Her scowl was visible even though the monitor was darkened. She took a deep breath and willed the Christmas spirit to enter her body. When she exhaled she tried to smile. What a miserable attempt.

Christmas was not her favorite time of year, and she was tired of being called Scrooge. She didn't want to be like this. It had been twenty-five years since her heart was broken during the Christmas holiday and she was over it. She'd been over it for a long time...at least that's what she kept telling herself.

A knock on the door brought her back to her purpose. That would be Declan Sommerfield, here for his weekly check-in. She had been his counselor since he walked onto campus back in August for his first semester as a student athlete at Denison University. He had taken her suggestions and had excelled academically this first semester which could sometimes be difficult for freshmen. She had immediately liked the young man and couldn't put her finger on why, but there was something familiar about him.

"Come in."

A tall, lanky, sandy haired young man came through the door. "Hi Coach Markus."

Makenna shook her head at the greeting. "Declan, how many times do I have to tell you I'm not a coach?"

"You are to me," he said, sitting down on the couch in her office.

Makenna got up from her desk and came around to the chair opposite the couch. "How's your week been? Are you ready for the Christmas break?"

"I'm ready for classes to be over, but you know I'll have practice during the entire break."

"You'll get some time off. I thought you were going home for Christmas," she said, a bit concerned.

"I was, but my mom has decided to come here for the holidays," he said, seeming unaffected.

"Are you disappointed you're not going home?"

"Not at all. Christmas has never been a very cheery time around my family."

"Really? I can relate. It's not my favorite." Makenna shifted uncomfortably in her chair. "What else is going on?"

"I got my grades in all but one class. I'll take that final tomorrow and then I'll be finished," he said happily.

"How did you do?"

"Don't you know?"

Makenna chuckled. "I could check, but I know you'll tell me. So, how did you do?"

"I have a B in Calculus and A's in everything else."

"That's awesome, Declan!" She got up and high-fived him.

"I should get an A in Creative Writing tomorrow unless I blow the final but I don't see that happening."

"I'm really proud of you."

Declan's smile beamed on his face. He didn't know why her opinion meant so much to him, but it did. "I couldn't have done it without you. Seriously *Ms.* Markus," he added.

Makenna laughed and shook her head. "You know you can call me Makenna."

"I know. It's too much fun keeping you guessing."

This kid, Makenna thought. "I'm glad your semester is ending well. Just so you know, I'll be here over the holiday if you need me."

"I'm sure I will. Do you do family counseling too? My family could probably use it."

Makenna furrowed her brow. He'd never mentioned problems with his family although he did tell her his parents were divorced and had been since he was four.

Declan noticed her concern. "It's okay. Hopefully it'll be me and my mom for the holidays. I'm sure my dad will spend the entire time with my other family. And Mom won't invite my grandparents, which I consider a gift."

"You don't get along with your grandparents?"

"Not really. It's more that my mom doesn't get along with them. They can be demanding and if you don't do things their way then it's not pretty. She wised up and the two of us do our own thing now."

"You're not staying in the dorm are you?"

"No. My mom was vague, which isn't unusual when talking about our family. But we're staying in a house that belongs to her somehow or another," he said, murmuring at the end.

"Okay," Makenna said, nodding and trying to follow his ramblings. "At least you won't be in the dorm."

"And my mom is a great cook so she'll be making me all sorts of treats and feeding me well. She makes the best pecan pie. I'll get her to make you one."

"How nice, Declan. But you don't have to do that."

"I'm telling you Coach, it's the best pecan pie you'll ever taste." Excitement covered his face and his eyes twinkled.

Those eyes and that smile touched a memory from the past that Makenna couldn't quite bring forward. It made her smile though and she could feel his happiness.

"That's certainly filled you with the Christmas spirit."

He looked around the room and then eyed her. "There's not much of it around here."

She looked around and saw how devoid her office was of

Christmas decorations, unlike the hall outside and the rest of the building. "What do you mean, there's a snow globe right there on the table in front of you."

Declan smirked and picked it up and shook it. "That's what I like about you. You're authentic and honest. Why decorate with a bunch of stuff if you don't feel it?" He set the globe down. "Seriously Makenna, I hope you have a happy holiday."

His candor made her smile and sit back in her chair. There was that twinkle in his eyes. "Thank you Declan." She looked down at her notes and back up at him, the moment having passed. "What do you have the rest of the day?"

"I have a little studying to do for tomorrow and then I'm packing a bag. My mom will be here tonight."

"All you have tomorrow is the one final?"

"Yes, but I also have a workout right down the hall in the weight room. I'll stop in and say hi. Hey, did I see you cranking on the spin bike the other day in the all purpose room?"

"You may have," she answered evasively then chuckled.

Declan laughed. "We should go run sometime."

"Oh, I don't think so. I couldn't keep up with you."

"I'll go slow," he offered.

"Listen," she began, needing to change the subject, "even though there aren't any classes, I'll be in and out. So if you need me, call or text."

"Thanks. You're not going skiing or seeing your family?"

"My family is right here, so I will be too."

"Okay. I'll text you when Mom makes your pie," he said as he got up.

"Good luck tomorrow," she said, walking him to the door. "Oh wait." She walked over to her desk and picked up a bowl of Christmas candy. "Here," she said, offering him the bowl. "I have a little Christmas cheer. Take all you want."

"Candy canes are my favorite," he said, taking several from the bowl.

"Bye Declan."

He smiled and took off down the hall.

Makenna closed her door and shook her head. If she ever had a son she'd want him to be like Declan Sommerfield.

2

Vanessa walked around the house as memories wrapped around her like a warm shawl. She could smell her grandmother's famous chocolate chip cookies cooling on the kitchen counter. As she walked through the living room she could hear the news on the TV that her grandfather watched every night. She remembered it came on at five, then five-thirty and then at six and she asked him why he watched it three times. Smiling, she could hear him say, "It takes three times for it to soak in."

Next she walked down the hallway to the room she slept in when she'd visited. Memories of Makenna nearly knocked her down. She remembered sitting on the bed and stealing a kiss, fearful her grandmother might walk in. The butterflies from all those years ago were fluttering again in her stomach because what she remembered next took her breath away.

Makenna had spent the night. When they were sure her grandparents were asleep they explored one another's bodies with tentative kisses and touches at first. But their courage grew with each quiet moan and labored breath. She could still feel the velvety softness of Makenna the first time she slid her finger inside. How could she still remember that? Surely it was because she was standing in the room where it happened.

She heard a car pull into the driveway. Shaking herself out of the past she walked to the living room and looked out the window. A smile grew on her face as she recognized her son's car. She opened the front door and waved.

He returned her wave, walking toward her with a bag thrown over his shoulder. "Hi Mom," he said, opening his arms for a hug.

"My boy!" she exclaimed and wrapped her arms around his waist, pulling him tight.

"Mom, really? I'm not a boy."

"Come on Declan. You'll always be my boy. And I'm happy to see you," she said, walking him into the house with her arm still around his waist.

"Wow!" he said, looking around. "Dated much?"

Vanessa chuckled. "I know. I opened up a few windows earlier so it could air out some but it got chilly in here."

"So explain to me again how this is your house."

"Well, my grandparents, Gran's mom and dad, lived here. I came to visit summers and holidays when I was younger. I spent the entire summer here right before I went off to college."

"How horrible was that?" he asked, walking around the living room looking at the old pictures on the end tables.

She laughed and then quieted. "It wasn't horrible at all. It was one of the best summers ever."

Declan looked at her curiously as her voice trailed off. "Mom? What was so great?"

Vanessa brought herself back to the present. "Oh, you know how your Gran is. I was away from her, that's what made it great."

"I can definitely understand that." He laughed with her.

"So, enough about the past. Do you have to study?"

"Nope. I looked over everything for tomorrow's final after my counseling appointment this afternoon. That reminds me, would you make my counselor one of your awesome pecan pies? I couldn't have made it through the semester without her."

"Is this the academic counselor your coach set you up with that you're always talking about?"

"I'm not always talking about her. She was really helpful with adjusting to college life and athletics. It was really stressful there for a while. But with her help I should bring home all A's and one B."

"Way to go, honey. I'm proud of you."

"Thanks Mom. So will you bake her a pie? I told her how good yours are."

"I'd be happy to. But tonight we're eating out because there's no food in this place. I'll go to the grocery store tomorrow."

"Works for me."

"This is your turf so you pick. What do you want to eat?"

* * *

Makenna pulled into her driveway and saw a black blur dart across the yard. She smiled, knowing it was one of her two cats welcoming her home even though she was a little later than usual. A quick workout had turned into a longer one when she felt like she was in the zone. She chuckled to herself recalling Declan Sommerfield's invitation to run with him.

She walked into the house as the blur scurried through the open door. A chorus of meows greeted her as she closed the door and walked into the kitchen. "My goodness you act like I never feed you. Come here Tina, you beautiful ball of fur." The cat came over and walked between her legs as Makenna bent down to pet her. She was a black fluffy cat with orange and red highlights. Makenna had never seen another cat look like her.

She purred with every stroke until she was bumped out of the way by a bigger yellow and white cat. "Max, don't be mean to your little sister." Makenna pet them both to growls and purrs. "Okay, here's your food." She filled both their bowls and watched them for a minute. "I'm the typical lesbian with cats," she said out loud and laughed at herself.

She looked in her refrigerator and found nothing to make much of a dinner for herself. Next she opened the pantry and didn't find anything there either. She released a big breath and walked back to her room to change clothes. She threw on a sweatshirt and a pair of joggers and put her hair in a ponytail, pulling it through her favorite cap.

On the way back to the kitchen she stopped at the hall closet and pulled out a coat. "I'll be right back, kids. Momma needs some supper."

She could hear a noodle bowl with sweet and spicy cauliflower from her favorite Vietnamese restaurant calling her name. Her favorite place was in an area full of restaurants and nightlife so she called her order in on the way. All she'd have to do is hop out, run in and pick it up.

A car was backing out just as she pulled into the area of the restaurant and she felt fortunate because they were busy tonight. People meandered up and down the walkway. She jumped out, locked her car and ran into the restaurant. The aromas that assaulted her nose made her stomach growl.

"Hi Makenna. How are you this evening?"

"Hey Jason. I'm hungry and wanted you to cook for me tonight."

"I'm happy to do it," he said, laughing. "Let me get your order."

"Thanks." She looked around and saw a few students that she recognized from campus. The live music in the background almost made her want to stay for a while.

"Here you go," he said, placing a bag on the counter as he rang up her order.

"Thanks Jason." She handed him cash from her pocket. "Keep the rest for you."

"Aw thanks Makenna. Enjoy your evening."

"I will now," she said, her eyes wide. She grabbed the bag and walked out the door.

She walked in front of the restaurant and was about to step off the curb when she heard "Hey, Coach Markus!"

Makenna turned and saw Declan Sommerfield walking toward

her, his face bright with a smile. A woman was just behind him, trying to keep up.

"Hey Declan," she said, returning his smile.

"I'm so glad we ran into you. I want you to meet my mom," he said, turning to the woman that walked up beside him.

Makenna's mouth fell open. She'd know her anywhere. It may have been twenty-five years, but she'd always recognize the woman that took her heart, who was now standing next to Declan. She was even more beautiful than the memories burned into Makenna's brain.

"Vanessa?" she said, not trusting her eyes.

Vanessa looked up and stopped in her tracks. "Makenna, is that you? Of course it's you!" she said, suddenly breathless.

"You know each other," Declan said, confused but smiling.

They were both visibly surprised, but neither said anything nor looked away for a long moment.

"I can't believe it," Vanessa whispered. A smile began to take over her face as her eyes sparkled.

That's when Makenna realized why Declan's eyes seemed so familiar. They were Vanessa's! And she couldn't stop looking into them. How many times had she fallen into those rich amber eyes?

Vanessa cleared her throat, unable to stop smiling. "We knew each other a long time ago."

Makenna finally looked away and smiled up at Declan. "Showing your mom your favorite hangouts?"

"Not really. There's no food in the house."

Makenna nodded and turned to Vanessa. "Are you staying at your grandparents' place?"

"Yeah," she said softly as she tried to hold Makenna's gaze. "It's actually mine now."

Hearing this, Makenna's eyes widened. "Yours?"

"Yeah, they're both gone now and they actually left it to me."

Makenna nodded, remembering Vanessa's grandparents. "I'm sorry, they were really nice people."

Vanessa nodded in agreement, but could only stare at Makenna's deep brown eyes, trying to read her thoughts.

"Well, it's nice to see you again, Nessa. Good luck on your final tomorrow, Declan."

"Thanks, Coach. I'll drop by and see you," he said with a grin.

She turned to walk away when Vanessa reached out and gently grabbed her arm. "It was great seeing you, Ken."

Makenna couldn't help but smile. "It's good to see you too, Nessa."

Vanessa dropped her hand and Makenna walked into the parking lot. Vanessa stared after her as Declan's voice broke the moment.

"I can't believe you know each other. That is so cool!"

"I can't believe Makenna Markus is the counselor you've been talking about all this time," she murmured, still watching Makenna walk away.

"Come on. I'm hungry."

"Me too." She followed Declan into the Vietnamese restaurant.

"Find us a seat and I'll order. Okay?'

"All right," she said looking around. "I'm going to the back."

Vanessa found them a booth and sat down as she replayed the previous five minutes. For so many years, she'd dreamed of finding Makenna. All she needed was a chance. A chance to apologize for her cowardice, for not coming to find her when she finally got out of her marriage. But then she had Declan. This wasn't exactly how she may have dreamed it, but she was here and she could see with one look that Makenna Markus still loved her. All she needed was a chance.

3

Makenna couldn't stop thinking about last night. It was supposed to be a simple trip to one of her favorite places to get supper. The whirlwind that was Vanessa Perry, or whatever her name was now, had stormed back into her life and now she couldn't think of anything else.

She leaned back in her office chair and closed her eyes. Last night she'd been so shocked she couldn't speak, but today she could visualize Vanessa's thick curly hair gleaming in the lights from the shops and her bright twinkling amber eyes looking into her soul. She shuddered remembering how exposed she'd felt and how much she'd wanted to walk right into those arms that had held her so long ago.

Makenna stopped herself and opened her eyes abruptly as she sat up. What was she thinking? This woman had broken her heart and as much as she hated to admit it, as hard as she'd tried, she hadn't gotten past it. Last night was proof that Vanessa still had a hold on her like no one ever had. What was wrong with her? They weren't kids anymore; she was an adult, a reasonable adult that counsels kids growing into adults.

A knock on the door stopped the battle raging inside her. She shook her head and released a deep breath. "Come in."

Vanessa walked through the door holding a box. "So it's Dr. Markus now. May I come in?"

Makenna got up and walked around her desk, her heart immediately thumping in her chest. "For as long as I went to school, my degree had to come with something. A title and some letters were the prize."

Vanessa walked over to the couch and set the box on the table next to the snow globe.

"Have a seat," said Makenna, sitting on the end of the couch, hoping her nervousness wasn't plain to see.

Vanessa sat down in the middle and turned toward Makenna. She seemed unsure of herself and then reached for the box, holding it out. "I baked you a pie."

Makenna smiled and took the box, relaxing somewhat. "That Declan. You didn't have to do that."

"I should warn you that it's not pecan. I remembered my grandmother made a cherry pie once that you were wild about it. It's her recipe." Vanessa smiled mischievously. "Don't tell Declan. He asked for pecan."

"Thank you." Makenna visibly softened, remembering that day from so many years ago. She tilted her head. "And yes, I'm still wild about cherry pie."

"I want to thank you for all you've done for Declan. He swears he wouldn't have made it through the semester without you."

"You're welcome. He's a great kid. We hit it off from the start so it's been a joy working with him."

Vanessa put her arm on the back of the couch and quietly said, "He's the one thing I've done right in my life, Kenna."

Makenna smiled and nodded, setting the pie back on the table.

"I have so many things I want to tell you, Ken," she continued, narrowing her eyes.

"Vanessa, it was such a long time ago." Color rushed to Makenna's cheeks, which always happened when Vanessa was near.

"I know and I know what I did to you. I know what I did to us."

For a long moment they stared into one another's eyes, weighing their options, assessing the risks.

Finally Vanessa blurted out, "Let me cook for you."

"What?" Makenna asked, not sure of what she heard.

"It's what I do. After the divorce I threw myself into cooking and it's what I do now."

"Declan said you would feed him well while you were here," she said, chuckling.

"Ken, come to the house. Let me cook for you and—" Vanessa broke off, searching for the right words. "Just come and spend a little time with me. Please, Kenna."

Makenna didn't know why she was hesitating. She had never been able to say no to Vanessa Perry and wasn't about to now. A slow smile formed on Makenna's face. "Okay, Nessa."

Vanessa breathed a sigh of relief and her face beamed with the idea that soon she and Makenna would be back in her grandparent's house. This was her chance.

Someone knocking on the door startled them both.

Makenna said, "Come in."

Declan's face peered around the opening door. "Hey Coach Markus." He walked into the room and was surprised to see his mom sitting on the couch. He saw the box on the table and smiled. "Mom brought you a pie. Have you tasted it yet? I'm telling you, it's the best."

Makenna looked at Vanessa and they both laughed.

"No, I haven't tasted it yet, but I know it will be delicious," she said, giving Vanessa a knowing smile. Then she turned back to Declan. "How was your final?"

"I'm quite sure it's another A."

Makenna got up and high-fived him. "Way to go! I'm proud of you."

"I am too," Vanessa said.

"Thank you both," he said, giving them a slight bow.

Vanessa cleared her throat. "I was just asking Makenna to come to dinner."

"Great! Tonight?" Declan asked excitedly.

"Um well," Makenna stammered, looking at Vanessa.

"I'd love for you to come tonight." Vanessa gave Makenna a hopeful look. "Oh wait. Is there someone you want to bring? I mean, I don't know if, or..." She let the statement hang awkwardly.

Makenna smiled, rescuing her. "No, it's just me, Nessa. And sure, I can come tonight."

"Oh cool. Coach!"

"How about six?" Vanessa smiled, hoping she didn't look as nervous as she felt.

"Six it is."

* * *

Makenna pulled into the driveway and memories came flooding back. She'd driven by this house from time to time, but tonight she knew Vanessa was in there and waiting on her. The thought made the butterflies she'd had off and on all day take flight. She'd been asking herself all afternoon what she was doing. It was foolish to think that there was something still between them. But then why did she change outfits several times before settling on the black jeans and deep periwinkle blue sweater that complemented her chestnut brown hair and eyes? Makenna shook her head. Vanessa probably just wanted to thank her for working with Declan.

As she walked toward the front door it sprang open and Vanessa stood there smiling. Her long, curly auburn hair fanned out over her shoulders and trailed down her back. It looked like a fiery halo with the lights from the house in the background.

Makenna paused, drinking in her beauty, and almost forgot to breathe. She returned her smile and closed the distance between them. She noticed that Vanessa was wearing an apron. This surprised her a little, but she didn't know why.

Vanessa must have seen her expression change because she looked down and then back up at Makenna. She raised her eyebrows and playfully said, "I'm a very messy cook and didn't want to ruin my sweater." *Which I chose specifically for you* she thought, but didn't share. "What do you have there?" she asked, noticing the wrapped bottle in Makenna's hands.

"Oh, I brought wine." She held out the bottle.

"Aw, thanks Ken. Come on in. Be ready for a blast from the past. I haven't done any updates yet." She stepped aside so Makenna could walk through the door. Vanessa could smell Makenna's hint of perfume and wanted to reach out and touch her, but she refrained for now.

"Oh wow, you weren't kidding," she said, turning to Vanessa. "It's like walking back in time."

"Have you ever wanted to do that, Ken?" asked Vanessa softly. "Go back?"

Makenna locked eyes with Vanessa and took a deep breath. Declan walked in before she could answer.

"Hey Coach Markus," he said, walking over to them. He noticed the bottle in his mom's hand and took it from her, looking at the label. "Wine, huh. You and mom can share this and reminisce about the good old days," he said with a laugh.

"We can," Vanessa said. "Let's go in the kitchen and get this opened. Dinner is not quite ready."

Makenna followed Declan into the kitchen, very aware of Vanessa behind her. She had to calm down or she'd never make it through this night.

"Have a seat," Vanessa said, gesturing toward the table in the kitchen. "Declan, take Makenna's coat, please."

She took her coat off and handed it to Declan as she watched Vanessa open the wine. Her hands worked like they had done the task dozens of times.

Declan came back in and leaned against the counter. "So, what did you two do back in the day?"

"Well, just what regular kids did back then," Vanessa said, glancing at Makenna and remembering hot kisses shared in a car on a secluded road.

Makenna recalled soft caresses under the covers in the dead of night in Vanessa's bedroom right down the hall. "Yeah, like regular kids."

"Actually I met Makenna down at the river."

Makenna smiled; she could still remember the curvy redhead with long legs in short shorts sauntering up to her.

"At the river?"

"Yeah, they had this event. I guess it was kind of like a festival with food and games. There was an area roped off where kids could swim and Makenna was the lifeguard," Vanessa explained, looking at Makenna and seeing the tan, sandy blond muscular lifeguard that she walked up to and had to meet.

"Your mom walked right up to me and introduced herself. We hit it off and spent the summer together after that." Makenna smiled at Vanessa, the happy memories hanging in the air with an ominous storm far off in the distance they both knew now was coming.

"That was when I first learned to cook. I would spend the day with Mimi cooking for Pops while Makenna worked at the pool, and then every evening we were up to something." She looked over at Makenna, those eyes twinkling.

"What happened? You never came back?" asked Declan.

Makenna spoke up, her voice soft. "You came back that Christmas."

"Yeah," Vanessa said, a far off look in her eyes. "Remember when we found that Christmas Stroll in that little town not far from here?"

"I remember," Makenna said quietly with a sad smile, her eyes never leaving Vanessa's.

Declan looked from his mom to Makenna, then back to his mom. "That's it? You never came back?"

"You know, Declan, it's kind of a long story that I'm going to tell you about, but not tonight. This is a happy night."

"You can't leave me hanging like that, Mom," he said, exasperated.

"I'll tell you this much. Your grandparents kept us apart. They wouldn't let us see each other."

Declan looked at his mom, trying to figure out what she wasn't saying. "Why? I knew Gran could be a bitch, but damn, Mom."

"Declan!" Vanessa scolded half-heartedly. "You can't talk about your grandmother like that."

He looked at his mom and could see she wasn't going to say any more right now.

"Pie, Declan!" Makenna interjected, trying to change the subject. "I need to tell you about the pie."

Declan tore his eyes away from his mom and looked at Makenna. A smile grew on his face as he said, "Best thing your mouth has ever tasted, wasn't it!"

Makenna choked on her wine. After coughing she said, "Yes, it was heavenly." She could hear Vanessa laughing under her breath, but knew better than to look at her.

"I told you!" Declan said, not noticing the moment between his mom and Makenna.

"But what I need to tell you is that it was not pecan."

Confused, Declan looked at her and waited.

"Your mom remembered that I loved her grandmother's cherry pie so that's what she made me." Looking at Vanessa she said, "It was as good, if not better than your Mimi's."

"Oh good. It had been a long time since I'd made one."

"Well lucky for you Mom made a pecan too."

"That's right. We're having it for dessert."

"Can't wait," Makenna said.

"Okay you two, come fill your plates, we're doing this buffet style. I'll bring your drinks to the table."

After they had filled their plates and sat down to eat, Declan began to catch Vanessa up on some things he hadn't shared during the semester. Makenna clarified or added to the stories when Declan asked. There was a happy banter between Vanessa and Declan like they'd done this many times and Makenna fit right in the flow.

"This was delicious, Vanessa. These shrimp tacos taste just like you grilled them outside." Makenna groaned with delight.

Vanessa smiled, her thoughts going to other times she'd heard that very sound from Makenna. "I'm glad you like it, I wasn't sure what to make. I thought I'd bring a little summer into this winter evening. These remind me of those tacos we used to get at that little place not far from the pool."

"They do."

"Is it still there?" Vanessa asked.

"It is. We'll have to go while you're here," Makenna said, surprising herself as well as Vanessa.

"That'd be nice." Vanessa nodded. "Okay, who's ready for pie?" She hopped up and took their plates and brought the pie back over.

As she cut the pieces and served it on plates she said, "I'm a little nervous. Declan has talked this up so much, I hope it's good. You never know."

Declan and Makenna both moaned on the first bite. Vanessa smiled, taking that as a compliment.

"He's right, this is amazing." Makenna moaned again as she took another bite.

"I'm glad you like it," Vanessa said. She'd cooked for a lot of people over the years and was always pleased when they appreciated her food, but this was so much more. Pleasing Makenna in this small way filled her heart. She knew right then she would do whatever it took to keep Makenna Markus in her life.

Declan finished his pie in three bites. "Wow! Are we keeping you from something?"

Vanessa commented on his manners.

"Sorry. It's really good, Mom. But I'm going to leave you two to reminisce because I'm going to Tyler and Ryan's to play video games." He picked up his plate and put it in the sink as Vanessa and Makenna both watched him.

He held up his hand, palm out. "Mom, let's not embarrass us both. I've been here for several months now and haven't gotten into any trouble."

Vanessa raised her eyebrows but before she could say anything Makenna spoke up. "But what kind of parent would she be if she didn't say keep making those good choices you've been making over the last several months?"

Declan threw his head back and laughed. "Well played Makenna, well played."

Makenna laughed, noticing he called her by her first name.

"Have fun," Vanessa said, laughing. She loved observing the relationship that Declan and Makenna had built.

"See you later, Coach. Bye Mom." And with that he went out the back door and was gone.

Makenna shook her head and chuckled. "He's so much like you."

"What do you mean?"

"He's like a little tornado that sweeps in and then he's gone," she said, smiling.

"Is that what I am? A tornado that swept in and wrecked your life?"

Makenna looked into Vanessa's eyes. "I always thought of you as a whirlwind. But you didn't wreck my life."

They held one another's gaze.

4

"Let me help you clean up," Makenna said, abruptly standing up and grabbing plates.

They went to the sink and began washing the dishes. Vanessa handed a clean, rinsed plate to Makenna to dry. Their fingers touched as Makenna took the plate, but Vanessa didn't let go. "I want to tell you what happened."

Makenna looked at her and waited.

Vanessa let the plate go. "I'm sorry I wasn't stronger back then."

"Vanessa, I remember how scary your mother was."

"Yeah, and she still is. Anyway, after I left here and went back home they watched me like a hawk. I did what was expected and knew they'd let me go back to school. I figured that once I was back there I would be able to contact you and we could figure out what to do. I missed you so much and my heart was broken, but I knew it wouldn't be long until I could talk to you. I just had to hang on." Vanessa paused to take a breath, remembering the awful hole in her heart.

"My heart was broken too," Makenna said softly.

Vanessa stopped and looked at her. "Oh Ken," she said with tears in her eyes. She took a breath and continued. "The day I was set to go back to school, she told me that she knew what I was planning to do. She said she would find out if I contacted you. And if I did, she would go to your parents and even to your school and tell them. I couldn't believe it! I thought about what you said that night about your parents maybe understanding, but when she said she'd go to your school—I don't know, Kenna, I couldn't risk ruining your life like that because people can be so cruel." She took a big breath. "So, I told her I was going to write to you and tell you not to contact me because I knew you would try to and I didn't want her to ruin your life, too."

"Wow," was all Makenna could say. *She was protecting me.* That thought kept going through her head.

"She was so evil, Makenna. It really scared me. I could see that she was going to do whatever she could to make your life miserable and I couldn't do that to you. At that point, I didn't care about me, but I had to protect you."

It was a lot to take in and Makenna let Vanessa's words swirl around her brain and her heart. She kept coming back to Vanessa's statement that she was protecting her.

"Ken, are you all right? You're not saying anything."

Makenna realized that Vanessa was finished with the dishes and putting the food away. Vanessa reached over and gently took the dish that Makenna had been drying for the last five minutes.

She smiled kindly. "I think this one is dry." Vanessa stacked it with the others in the cabinet. "Let's sit in the living room. Would you like more wine?"

Makenna nodded. Vanessa topped off their glasses and Makenna followed her into the living room. They both sat on the couch, keeping some distance between them.

Makenna looked into Vanessa's eyes. When she had arrived there was hope in her eyes and excitement that they were together again. But now, Makenna thought she saw pain and hurt. She couldn't stop the emotions running through her and the pain in those eyes went straight to her heart.

"You were protecting me. God, Nessa. I didn't reach out to you because I was afraid they'd lock you away somewhere." Makenna shook her head and looked away. "Your mother was a master at manipulation. She knew we would protect one another and she made it work to keep us apart."

"She did."

Makenna let out a deep breath. "What happened next? I mean, I guess it's not any of my business, but you do have Declan and I know you were married."

Vanessa took a sip of her wine and set her glass on the table. She turned toward Makenna and their knees touched. Neither of them moved away. The simple contact seemed to calm them both as the sad memories hung in the room.

"I concentrated on school. I was still in the sorority because my mother insisted, but I did the minimum. Whenever I saw a girl with long blond hair I thought it was you. By the time I was a senior I'd given up on trying to find you. One weekend when I knew my parents were out of the country on vacation, I came here and even drove by your house."

Makenna's face lit up. "You did?" She chuckled. "I used to drive by this house all the time, hoping to catch just a glimpse of you."

"Mother never let me come back here. My grandparents always came to our house for holidays or visits after that."

Makenna shook her head, emotions bubbling inside of her at the senselessness of it all.

"My mother constantly pressured me to find a boyfriend. I was able to fend her off with my grades, claiming that I was busy studying and didn't have time to date. But there was one guy that was my friend. That was all. I knew he wanted to be more so I would go to special occasions with him as my date when I had to. My parents approved of him and again my mother pulled me aside and told me in no uncertain terms that I would never be with you or any other woman."

"So, this is Declan's dad?"

Vanessa nodded. "What upsets me the most now is that if I would have just had a little courage then, I could have gotten away. She made me believe that I couldn't make it on my own without them or without Daniel, Declan's dad."

"But you wouldn't have Declan," Makenna said, stating the obvious.

"Exactly. I liked Daniel. He was a nice guy and I thought that if this was the life I had to live then at least I'd be living with a friend. We got married when I graduated and I had Declan when I was twenty-four. We had a couple of good years, but Daniel knew I didn't love him." She paused and looked Makenna in the eyes. "He knew there was someone else in my heart."

Makenna looked into those amber eyes that were glistening with tears, but she saw deeper into Vanessa's heart and could see she still loved her.

"We divorced when Declan was four. I jumped into cooking because it reminded me of my grandmother and you. My mother tried to continue to run my life, but when I told her I wouldn't let her see Declan she backed off."

Makenna's eyebrows shot up her forehead at this declaration.

"I wanted to find you so badly then, but I convinced myself that you had forgotten all about me and were probably living a happy life. Plus I had Declan."

Makenna sat back, taking all this in.

"After the divorce I took my marketing degree and my skill in the kitchen and found a job with one of those meal delivery services. And that's what I'm doing today."

"So much is going through my head," said Makenna.

"I can imagine. When your school recruited Declan I couldn't believe it. Well, I didn't know that you worked there until yesterday."

"You didn't?"

"No, I didn't even think you were still in town. Whenever he talked about you, which was nearly every time I talked to him, he'd call you Coach or Marcus. I didn't even know you were a woman for months."

Makenna shook her head. "I knew there was something familiar about him from the first day I met him. But I couldn't put my finger on it. There was something in the past that would tug at me and now I know. It's that twinkle in his eyes, just like yours, and the way he takes over a room, just like you."

"When I brought him to school back in August I drove by your house again. And I came by here. God, I sound like some lovesick teenager."

"We were," Makenna said softly.

"Yeah, we were. Can you ever forgive me, Ken?"

"Forgive you for what?"

"For being weak. For having a horrible mother."

"Vanessa, I've met your mother. You were young I can see how she made you think you didn't have a choice."

"You look angry."

"I am," Makenna admitted. "I'm angry that you thought I didn't come find you because I'd forgotten you. I'm angry at myself for thinking you didn't care because your mother couldn't stand the idea you were a lesbian." Makenna got up and paced the room. She stopped and looked at Vanessa. "Can you imagine what a wonderful life we could've had? I mean, maybe we wouldn't have made it, but at least we would have had a chance."

"But we've found each other again, Kenna," Vanessa said shakily.

Makenna smiled, but it didn't reach her eyes. She really wanted to take Vanessa in her arms, but so much time had passed. And what happened when the holidays were over and Vanessa went back to her life? Makenna didn't want to relive that heartache ever again.

"Would you tell me what happened to you after I left?"

Makenna sat back down and took a deep breath. "After you left, I cried enough to increase the level in the river to flood stage. I'm not trying to be funny, Nessa. That's what it felt like. To hear the fear in your voice that night and in your letter made me afraid too. So, I held on until graduation. By then I was ready to get out of here. But things didn't work out for me to go away to college so I stayed here. I guess it was in my junior year that the idea of hiding who I am hurt more than anything coming out could do to me."

"That is so brave," Vanessa said in awe, her voice barely audible.

Makenna smiled, remembering how it felt to release that burden. It was surely a mental and emotional relief, but also physical. Her entire being had blossomed.

"Just as my brother told me, my parents were understanding and fine with it. One time not too long after that my mom asked me about you. She knew I was hurting and didn't know what to do about it. I explained to her what happened and if she could've talked to your mom I think she would have. But I begged her not to because I had no idea what your mother would still do to you even though it was years later."

"That must be an amazing feeling to have your parents' support. I think that's why I've always assured Declan that no matter what he wanted to do I was behind him."

"I could tell that in my conversations with him."

"This may be none of my business, but Kenna, what about girl-friends? Have you been married?"

Again Makenna attempted to smile. Vanessa looked at her nervously, wanting to know, but also afraid of what she might hear.

"There have been girlfriends. I've had two relationships that lasted any length of time. One was three years, the other five. A couple of years after we broke up, one of my exes sat me down and told me that the real reason she left is because I hid the most precious part of me, a piece of my heart that only one person could reach. She wanted all of me and knew she'd never get it."

Vanessa's eyes burned into her soul. She was the one person that could have all of Makenna. But Makenna was unsure; the risk was too great. If it were just the two of them, she'd chance it because she knew they could make it. But what about Vanessa's mother, what about Declan, and realistically they didn't know each other anymore. Twenty-five years is a long time for a person to grow and change.

Vanessa could see the uncertainty in Makenna's eyes. She reached out and took her hand. "Do you remember the last thing I said to you?"

Makenna's heart skipped a beat when Vanessa took her hand. Shakily she replied, "Of course I remember."

"I do, Ken. I've loved you always."

Makenna let out a breath and tilted her head. She squeezed Vanessa's hand. "But Vanessa, we don't even know each other now."

"You know me, Kenna. I'm the same girl that was madly in love with you then and always have been. And I know you still love me. I can see it in your eyes."

Makenna smiled but was still hesitant.

"Give us a chance," Vanessa spoke hurriedly and as if her life depended on it because to her, it did. "Let's get to know one another again. I'll be here over the entire break." She tried not to squeeze Makenna's hand too hard. She wasn't letting Makenna leave without knowing she'd get to see her again. Her heart knew they were meant for one another.

Makenna's heart knew it too. She wanted this. She wanted Vanessa more than she'd ever wanted anything. That hadn't changed and never would. "But what about Declan?"

This didn't surprise Vanessa. She could see how much Declan and Makenna respected and cared for one another. "I'm telling Declan what happened between us and how I feel about you when he gets home tonight. I wanted him to see us together so it would be easier to explain."

"Seeing us together makes it easier?"

"Yes. It's obvious to me how good we can be together."

Makenna released a breath she didn't realize she'd been holding. She was still unsure but she couldn't resist the pull of this woman. "Okay then. Would you like to go to Leo's with me? We'll see if their tacos are as good as we remember."

The biggest smile filled Vanessa's face. She'd go anywhere with Makenna and this was her chance. "I'd love to. Tomorrow?"

Makenna chuckled. "Tomorrow it is. Nothing like jumping right in."

Vanessa scooted closer to Makenna and put her hand gently on her face. "I'm not wasting any time with you. Ever."

Makenna leaned into her hand. Her heart was beating out of her chest, but at the same time she felt a sense of calm at Vanessa's touch. "I'd better go."

Vanessa wanted to keep her there, but knew it was best to let her process everything that had been said. "I'll get your coat." Vanessa hopped up and took Makenna's coat off the chair across the room. She held it out so Makenna could slip it on. The small gesture filled her heart. "Come on, I'll walk you to your car," she said, opening the door and holding out her hand.

Makenna didn't hesitate and took her hand as they went through the door and walked to the car. Memories of that night at the Christmas Stroll were in the front of her mind when Vanessa spoke.

"I always loved holding your hand." She bumped her shoulder against Makenna's.

The gesture made Makenna's heart melt. She had to get out of here before all her defenses were gone.

Vanessa opened her car door. Makenna started to get in but stopped and turned to face Vanessa. "Thank you for dinner, Nessa."

"Anytime," she said smoothly and then gently placed her lips on Makenna's cheek in a lingering kiss.

Makenna got into the car and waited as Vanessa walked back into the house. She waved as she slowly closed the door. Makenna reached up and touched her cheek that was on fire from Vanessa's lips. She couldn't wait for tomorrow night.

5

The next day, Makenna was glad she didn't have to go into her office. There was no way she could concentrate. Luckily, during the holiday break she could set her own hours and wasn't required to be there. She found that with no students around it gave her time to catch up on recent literature published in her field, as well as prepare for next semester.

But today all she could think about was Vanessa. Knowing that Vanessa was protecting her when she wrote that last fateful letter didn't necessarily ease the pain she'd felt back then. At first she understood why Vanessa had stayed away because her parents provided everything for her and she was still in school. But why hadn't she come to find Makenna after she'd graduated?

Would it really have made a difference? By then Makenna had come out and was sleeping around, trying to erase the pain she still felt three years later. She was afraid to give her heart to anyone because the one time she had it had been broken to pieces. But finally, she began to forget and took a chance.

She had been reliving and remembering her past relationships all day and had finally come to the conclusion that she had given Vanessa her heart twenty-five years ago and hadn't been able to give it to anyone else. It was so much easier to help other people with their feelings and emotions and give them tools to use to make healthy decisions and understand why and what they were feeling. But she could never do that for herself. She would lie to herself, thinking she was all right. But when her ex had kindly explained why she left, Makenna had taken a hard look inside her heart and stopped lying to herself.

Since then there hadn't been anyone else. She would occasionally go out with women her friends would set her up with and they might have sex, but she hadn't even done that in a couple of years. Instead, she'd thrown herself into helping her student athletes.

And now here she was on her way to pick up Vanessa for an actual date. A date with the one person who had her heart, but Makenna was still afraid history might repeat itself. They were adults now and in control of their own lives. Was the love still there? It was for her, but was it enough for both of them to give up the lives they had now? Did Vanessa really control her own life or did her mother still have influence?

Makenna wrestled with these questions all day. She made up her mind when she left her house to stop those racing thoughts and try to enjoy this evening with Vanessa. She was not going to let the past ruin this evening and this chance to get to spend time with Vanessa as she got to know the woman she'd become. It was a big ask because of their history, but she wanted to know this Vanessa and she was sure Vanessa wanted the same. All she'd asked for was a chance and that's what Makenna was trying to do tonight: give them a chance.

She pulled into the driveway and saw both Declan and Vanessa's cars. A smile crossed her face as she thought of Declan and then butterflies attacked her stomach as she remembered Vanessa was going to tell him about them last night. She wondered if he would think of her differently. She was about to find out.

Before she could ring the doorbell Declan opened the front door. He had a big smile on his face. "Hey Makenna, come in."

Makenna raised her eyebrows in surprise at the greeting. He rarely called her by her first name. "Hi Declan. How's it going?"

"My first day without classes was great. I slept in and Mom and I watched a movie and I played video games. FYI, I did not work out today. It was recovery. Are you proud of me?"

They walked into the living room during Declan's update and Makenna turned to him in surprise. "You didn't go for a run or anything?"

"I did not."

"Good for you. I am proud. Now, make sure you don't do double tomorrow."

"You don't have to worry about that. Coach emailed us our work-outs for the next ten days and I always follow them to the letter."

Makenna smiled. "That's good."

"I think Mom is a little nervous about tonight," he said in a hushed voice.

Makenna's cheeks reddened and she started to fidget, shifting from one foot to the other.

Declan noticed and smiled. "Sorry. I don't mean to make you uncomfortable." He chuckled. "I guess this is a very important date for both of you."

Makenna released a deep breath. "It is. I don't know what all your mom told you, but I'm really happy for a chance to spend time with her again." She sighed, rubbing her forehead. "This is so awkward."

"Yeah, it kind of is, but it shouldn't be. We talk about everything, Coach."

"Yeah, everything about you. Not about me and your mom."

"Good point." They stood there in silence for a moment and then Declan said, "Well, here's what I think. My mom has been alone for a long time and she told me you were once in love. I can't think of a better person I'd want her to be in love with. So, I hope this works out for both of you."

Makenna was surprised. "Declan, I—"

"I know you're shocked. I may be a kid, but I noticed things growing up and my mom deserves to be happy."

"You're right, she does."

"She does what?" Vanessa said, walking into the room.

If Vanessa was beautiful at nineteen, she was absolutely stunning at forty-four. Her copper-colored hair cascaded down her shoulders in waves that landed below her collarbones. She was wearing black jeans that looked like they were made just for her. Her green loose fitting sweater was slouched over one shoulder and the peek of her collarbone made Makenna weak in the knees.

"Hey Mom, you look nice," Declan said, smiling.

"You sure do," Makenna said, her throat dry.

"Thank you both. Are you ready to go?"

Makenna found her voice and gazed into Vanessa's twinkling eyes. "I am."

They walked toward the door and Declan spoke up. "Now you kids don't be out too late."

They both stopped in their tracks. Vanessa looked over at Makenna with a grin. "I knew he'd have to say something."

Makenna nodded. "Of course he did."

Declan laughed in the background as Vanessa opened the door and they walked out. She grabbed Makenna's hand as they walked to the car. "I hope this is all right. You know how much I love holding your hand."

Makenna bumped her shoulder. "I love it too."

Vanessa bumped her back and then let her hand drop as she got in the car. Makenna walked around and got in, then drove them to the restaurant. Once inside and seated, they looked over the menu.

"Wow, I don't remember all these choices. Of course it's been a long time since I've been here," Vanessa said, still looking. "Would you want to share?" she asked, eyebrows raised and eyes twinkling.

"So that hasn't changed," Makenna said playfully. "I remember whatever was on my plate was yours too."

Vanessa pinned her with an amused look. "That's because you always said whatever was yours was mine."

Makenna laughed. "That's true, I did. You made every meal an event, an experience. It was always more than just food."

"It should be!" Vanessa exclaimed. "We're sharing more than food. We're sharing a moment in time we can't get back and we're sharing it with one another, no one else. That's special and should be treated that way."

Makenna melted a little inside listening to her, remembering how special every moment was when she was with Vanessa. "I would be happy to share with you." Makenna continued in a serious, more formal voice, "And I'd like to say I am extremely pleased to be spending and sharing this moment in time with you."

Vanessa smiled shyly at Makenna's tone and her heart swelled with hope. The waitress walked up before Vanessa could reply and asked if they were ready to order.

Makenna looked up at her and then pointed to the menu. "If possible, we'd like to get one of each of these tacos because we would like to share and create our own little taco-fest." She looked at Vanessa for approval and was rewarded with a smile that made her heart speed up.

"Sure, we can do that. I'll get them started." The waitress took their menus and walked toward the kitchen.

"That was genius," said Vanessa, thinking how much she'd like to kiss Makenna right that second. It must have shown on her face because Makenna's eyes darkened and she held her gaze as her lips parted slightly. Then she swallowed and looked away.

The moment passed and Vanessa leaned back in her chair, deciding to keep it light between them. "How was your day?"

A lazy smile played on Makenna's face. "It was nice not to go into the office. I love my job, but it can be intense at times. I'm always stressing the importance of recovery time to Declan."

"How so?"

"He likes to work out every day and thinks he's being lazy when he doesn't. So much so that he feels guilt. We've had several discussions on how recovery is just as important as skill work."

"Well, it's working because he didn't do anything today, unless you count gaming and watching movies. What did you do on your recovery day?" Vanessa tried to hide a slight smile because there were several times when she'd caught herself thinking about Makenna over the course of the day.

Makenna nodded slowly, thinking before answering. "I had a lot on my mind, processing information and emotions."

Vanessa let this sink in and carefully asked, "Since behavior and emotions are your job, do you find those skills to be helpful when you're dealing with feelings in your own life?"

Makenna chuckled. "Not at all. I can help these kids and their coaches through the toughest situations, but I'm as lost as they are sometimes when it comes to my own."

"You don't have any suggestions or behaviors to try when it comes to long lost first love?"

Makenna choked on the drink she was taking from her water glass.

While she recovered Vanessa continued. "The way I see it is that our hearts have been connected since the moment we met or we both wouldn't be sitting here in this moment about to share amazing tacos." Vanessa tapped lightly on her chest. "I think they are ecstatic at this chance. And now all they have to do is get the body and mind on the same page."

Makenna put her elbows on the table and rested her chin on her steepled hands as she contemplated Vanessa's theory. She appreciated her honesty and returned it. "From what I remember, our bodies never had a problem being on the same page and I think they still are."

Vanessa smiled seductively and said softly, "I agree."

The waitress brought their food, ending the intense moment to both their relief. She set the platter with the tacos in the middle of the table and gave them each a plate, refilling their glasses before she left.

They dug in and shared the tacos along with Vanessa's professional opinion and Makenna's personal one.

"What did you think of the shrimp?" Makenna asked.

"It's delicious, just as I remembered."

"Well, if I'm being honest, the one you prepared last night was better. This is good, but yours was out of this world." Makenna closed her eyes and remembered last night.

"That is a very kind thing to say and I respect your opinion. But taste this," Vanessa said, leaning over with a bite on her fork.

Makenna didn't hesitate because they had done this very same thing hundreds of times during that wonderful summer. "Mmm," she moaned. "That is so good. What is it?"

"They've taken this chicken and I think they slowly cooked it with lime and spices and then kissed it with cilantro right before serving it. I've tried this so many times, and mine is good, but they got this just right."

Makenna thought that this whole night had been just right.

"I don't think I could eat another bite," Vanessa said, putting down her fork. "This was a wonderful meal, but sharing it with you, Kenna, makes it unforgettable."

Makenna smiled at the sentiment and simply said, "Thank you, Ness."

They were silent for a few moments, gathering their thoughts as the waitress cleared the table.

"Did you want dessert?" Makenna asked.

"I'd love dessert, but I can't hold another bite."

"Well, maybe if you wait a bit you can. I happen to have a superb cherry pie made by a renowned chef at my house. If you're interested," she added.

Vanessa smiled and sat up excitedly. "I'd love to see your house."

"Okay, let's go."

6

After paying the bill, Makenna drove them to her house. They walked in and a chorus of meows supplied by Tina and Max greeted them.

"I think someone missed you," Vanessa said, watching the cats rub on Makenna's legs.

"Will you look at that," Makenna commented as Max made his way over and rubbed on Vanessa's legs.

"Does he not usually do that?"

"He doesn't warm up to people quickly. He must like you."

Vanessa leaned down and pet the cat. "Thanks buddy, I need all the help I can get."

Makenna chuckled. "Help?"

"Yeah, if he likes me, maybe that will soften you up and you'll give me a chance," she said playfully.

"I thought I was already giving *us* a chance," Makenna pointed out. "We did just have a great dinner. Correction," she said holding her hand up. "We just shared an experience that I only wanted to share with you."

Vanessa straightened up and moved closer to Makenna. "Really?

You only wanted to share with me?" Vanessa looked at Makenna's lips and then back into her eyes.

Makenna really wanted to kiss those lips that were plump and luscious and right in front of her. But the uncertainty of it all held her back. She swallowed and with a nervous smile, "Let me show you around."

Vanessa's face fell slightly, but she smiled and said sincerely, "Lead the way."

Makenna showed her through the living room and kitchen, commenting on what she'd redone and how it had looked when she moved in.

"How long have you lived here?"

"It's been about five years now." Makenna tilted her head, commenting as much to herself as Vanessa, "Wow, I didn't realize it'd been that long."

"Did you make the changes a little at a time or right after you moved in?"

"I painted and redid the floors when I moved in but I've replaced the kitchen cabinets and counters in the last year."

"I like what you chose. This kitchen may be on the smaller side, but you've used the space efficiently and made it easy to cook in. At least that's my opinion."

"You'd know. You're the chef. I just cook for me and occasionally for my family."

"Speaking of your family," Vanessa said, running her hand along the countertop, the quartz smooth under her touch. "Do you have big Christmas plans with them?"

"My parents are gone to my brother and his family's place right now, but they'll come back for Christmas Eve and Day here. My brother said it's too much hassle to bring all the presents for everyone and their kids here, so they'll open gifts Christmas morning and then come here for lunch."

"Are you going to your brother's too?"

"No. My nephews are teenagers now and although they agree

they have the coolest aunt on the planet, they would much rather be with their friends."

"I know exactly what you mean," Vanessa said, chuckling.

"I'll see them all when they come here, anyway." Makenna tilted her head toward the hallway. "Come on, I'll show you the rest." Makenna led them down the hall, showing Vanessa a guest bedroom and an office.

"Do you work a lot at home?"

"Oh, sometimes. It depends on what's going on with kids and if they are in season. It varies."

"Well, this is a sweet setup."

"Thanks." Makenna showed her a hall bathroom and then led her into her bedroom. Her heart began to speed up and she could feel her cheeks begin to color. She had dreamed of Vanessa in this bedroom the last two nights.

"Oh Kenna, this is lovely," she said, walking around the room. "It's peaceful and so you."

Makenna scoffed. "Now why would you say that?"

Vanessa wheeled around. "Oh, you don't think I know you? You think you're a different person than you were twenty-five years ago?"

"Of course I am in some ways."

Vanessa smiled. "Ken." She walked toward her.

Makenna's breath caught in her throat and then Vanessa walked right by and peeked into the master bath.

"I knew it. This is your favorite color—although it's toned down a little, it still counts," Vanessa said, sweeping her arm around the bathroom.

"Lucky guess," Makenna said, laughing.

That laughter was music to Vanessa's ears. "You always loved blue-green. You did then and you do now. It looks really good in here, by the way," she said, turning to Makenna as she stood in the door-way. Suddenly it felt a little tight in the room as it filled with expecta-tions. Vanessa took a deep breath and Makenna's eyes never left her. "You've done a beautiful job with the entire house, Kenna."

"Thanks," Makenna said a little breathlessly as she backed out of the bathroom.

"Would you want to help me redo my grandparents' place?"

"Hmm." Makenna stalled, walking toward the door. "Come on, I promised you this fantastic pie for dessert."

I know what I really want for dessert, Vanessa thought, watching Makenna walk down the hall. Was that a little strut in her step? Vanessa smiled. "You didn't answer me. Would you want to help me?"

Makenna cut the pie and put a slice for each of them on plates. "Are you redoing it to sell or to keep?" she asked, setting the plates on the table in the dining area.

Vanessa smiled again and decided to be honest. That was the only way she'd get Makenna back and that's what she wanted more than anything. She sat down and looked into Makenna's eyes across from her. "Well, when I first came back my thought was that I'd redo it and stay there when I came to see Declan, especially during his track season and his meets here."

Makenna forked a bite of her pie and put it in her mouth and then slowly slid the fork out. "And has that changed?"

Vanessa was mesmerized and watched every move Makenna made. At the sound of her voice she realized she'd asked a question. Vanessa gulped. "What was that?" She looked down at her own piece of pie and tried to gather herself.

"You said that was your plan when you first got here. Have your plans changed?"

Vanessa looked up and chewed the bite she'd slid in her mouth. After swallowing, she admitted, "My plans have changed because you're here."

Makenna sat up, surprised by Vanessa's honesty. "They have?"

"Yes. Do you think you'll stay here?"

Makenna's brow furrowed. "Stay here? Well, yeah. I love my job and the university. I get offers occasionally, but none compare to here. I haven't been here the whole time, Vanessa."

"What do you mean?"

"I went to undergrad here, but left to do my masters. Then I came back and got my PhD here. My mentor will be retiring in the next few years and I might think about moving into administration then."

Vanessa nodded and swallowed. "When I saw you two nights ago, my plans changed. I can do my job remotely, Kenna. There's nothing in the city for me. The two people that mean the most to me are here."

Makenna looked up, her eyes wide at this declaration. They had been toying with the idea of getting to know one another again, but this was a giant leap to something more.

"Don't look so afraid, Ken," Vanessa said with a smirk. "I know you feel it too."

"Vanessa," Makenna said, shaking her head. "It's not that easy. What happens when your mother finds out? What happens when your ex-husband finds out?"

"Do you hear yourself? I was the one that was afraid to be out back then, but I'm not now, Makenna. It doesn't matter what either of them say, I assure you."

"You say that now, Nessa. But you don't know what they could threaten you with."

"Oh Ken. There is nothing they can threaten me with. I am finally my own person. I'm just so sorry it took me this long. We've lost twenty-five years and I don't intend to lose even one more day with you."

Makenna wanted to believe her because she did feel the pull of Vanessa's heart and the push from her own. "What about Declan?"

Vanessa drew her eyebrows together. "Declan? He was fine with it." Vanessa took and released a breath. She scooted her chair over next to Makenna and took her hand. "We had a very long talk. He wondered why I never dated. And when I explained what happened to us and what we meant to one another it all made sense to him. I'm trying to remember how he put it." Vanessa wrinkled her nose in concentration. "He said we were his two favorite women and he couldn't be happier for us."

Makenna couldn't believe her ears. This just kept getting better, but the irony of it all made her laugh.

"What's so funny?"

"This is all moving so fast, but it's taken twenty-five years. That doesn't make sense."

Vanessa chuckled along with her. She reached up and ran the back of her fingers down Makenna's cheek. Sure there were a few wrinkles, but it only made her more beautiful. She ran her thumb over Makenna's bottom lip and lost her breath. But when she looked into Makenna's eyes they were almost black with desire and Vanessa could see her chest rising and falling.

She looked down at Makenna's lips, the same lips she had kissed so many times before. The lips that she dreamed about; the only lips she wanted. She leaned in and Makenna met her halfway. Softy, gently their lips touched and Vanessa knew she was home.

Makenna thought her heart would explode in her chest when her lips touched Vanessa's. They felt familiar and also new. She parted her lips slightly and Vanessa did the same. She sucked in her breath as their tongues met and it was the sweetest taste her mouth had ever experienced.

Vanessa's hands went to either side of Makenna's face just like they had hundreds of times all those years ago. It was as if their bodies remembered and their hearts too. Now all they had to do was let their minds catch up. But Vanessa couldn't think; all she could do was feel.

Makenna deepened the kiss as her tongue explored and a moan escaped her throat. Her hands found their way to Vanessa's shoulders and she pulled her closer. Vanessa groaned as their chests collided and she wrapped one arm around Makenna's back and the other she buried in her hair.

Vanessa pushed her way into Makenna's mouth and could taste the tartness of the cherries, but also the sweetness of Makenna. She was dizzy with desire and also pleasure from this long awaited kiss.

This kiss that spanned decades was full of want and need, but also hope. They didn't rush it. No, they fell into it and let the kiss take them where their hearts longed to be. Makenna slid her hands up and down Vanessa's back, relishing the feel of her long-ago lover.

Even with the fabric of her shirt separating her hands from Vanessa's soft skin, she remembered this feeling.

Vanessa ran her hands back along either side of Makenna's face and pulled back slightly before opening her eyes. Makenna stared back, but Vanessa looked down and her thumbs caressed the red and slightly swollen lips. She murmured, "I missed you so much." Then she claimed Makenna's lips once again with an intensity she hadn't felt in twenty-five years.

Makenna responded with equal fervor, never wanting the kiss to end. If it lasted twenty-five years it still wouldn't be long enough. A ping next to her ear barely registered and she kept kissing those lips, the lips that were her life now. And then there was the ping again. This time she realized it was Vanessa's watch. She pulled back, separating their lips, and Vanessa leaned in.

She murmured, "Un-huh." And their lips connected again. She felt Makenna smile and she smiled back, their lips still touching. Her watch pinged again.

Makenna couldn't ignore it any longer and pulled away. She didn't let Vanessa go, though. She raised her eyebrows in a silent question.

Vanessa looked into her eyes, in no hurry to check the watch. "That was..."

"Interrupted?"

She chuckled. "Sorry. It's Declan. No one else would be texting me." She paused and kept looking from Makenna's eyes to her lips and back. "I can't seem to stop looking at you."

Makenna giggled. "Why don't you see what he wants and then we can continue what we were doing."

Vanessa smiled. "Promise?"

"Promise," Makenna whispered, bringing their lips back together briefly.

Vanessa exhaled dramatically and looked at her watch. Her brows furrowed. "Let me get my phone." She got up and then immediately turned back around. "Don't you move."

Makenna laughed, watching her get her purse and find her

phone. Her forehead wrinkled and then she sighed. Makenna got up and walked over.

"Hey, you weren't supposed to move."

"Is everything all right?" she said, concerned.

"Yes," she said, sighing again. "It seems that Declan's dad decided to show up. He's at the house."

Makenna raised her eyebrows, her face full of questions.

Vanessa answered Declan's text and put her phone back in her purse. "I need to go to the house and see why he's here. Do you mind taking me home?"

"Of course not," Makenna said, turning to get her purse from the kitchen counter.

"Hey, this is just an interruption. Our date isn't over. Okay?"

Makenna nodded her head. "Okay," she said softly. They walked out and she drove them to Vanessa's grandparents' house.

7

W hen they pulled into the driveway Vanessa turned to Makenna. "Come in with me. This won't take long."

Makenna looked at her with surprise. "Are you sure?"

"Yes, I'm sure. I may need a favor. You'd help me, wouldn't you?" Vanessa opened the door and looked at Makenna, waiting for her answer before she got out of the car.

"Of course I'll help you," Makenna answered, opening her door and getting out.

They walked through the front door and found Declan sitting on one end of the couch, his father on the other.

Vanessa walked over to them boldly. She turned to make sure Makenna was behind her and smiled, feeling supported. "Makenna, I'd like for you to meet Declan's father, Daniel," she said, gesturing toward the man that was now standing.

"Hi Daniel," Makenna said, offering her hand.

Daniel took it. "Hi Makenna. Declan tells me you're one of his coaches."

"He likes to call me coach," she said, looking at Declan and smiling.

Daniel looked from Makenna to Declan, confusion on his face.

"Makenna is a sports psychologist," Declan explained. "She helps me keep my head right so I can improve my vaulting. I'm excited for the first meet because I'm feeling like this is going to be an exceptional season."

His confidence made Makenna smile. They had worked on his self-talk and speaking his truths like this into the universe. He acknowledged her smile and nodded his head.

"Daniel, did I miss something? What are you doing here?" Vanessa asked.

"Well, I got a concerned phone call from your mother."

Vanessa scoffed. "What? My mother?"

"We stay in touch occasionally. And she was concerned that you might be in a situation here that could harm Declan," he said, obviously uncomfortable.

"Harm me? We're having Christmas, Dad."

"Well, she was very cryptic. I thought I'd better come here and make sure you both were all right."

"Did you ever think about using that thing in your hand and calling or texting one of us instead of just showing up?" Vanessa asked sarcastically.

"Yes. But I wanted to see Declan anyway." He turned to his son. "Are you still coming to see us on Christmas Eve? The girls are beyond excited to see you."

"Yes Dad. I'm coming on Christmas Eve and spending the night. Then I'm coming back here to be with Mom Christmas night."

"Good," he said, relieved.

"Now back to my mother, Daniel. What was this about harming Declan?"

"W-well," he stuttered, obviously uncomfortable. "You know I'm an opened-minded person—"

"Hold up, Dad," Declan interrupted. "Mom, I need to talk to you real quick in here," he said, walking toward the kitchen. "Sorry Coach Markus, we'll be right back." Declan and Vanessa disappeared into the kitchen, leaving Makenna with Daniel.

"Uh, would you like to sit down?" Daniel motioned to the chair.

"Sure." Makenna sat in the chair next to the couch.

"Declan thinks the world of you. He was telling me some of the things you've taught him."

Makenna smiled. "He's a good student and athlete, but he's an even better person. I enjoy working with him because he isn't afraid to try new things, unlike some of the other freshmen that come to the university."

Daniel nodded his head and then tilted it at her curiously. "You're the one, aren't you?"

Makenna's brow furrowed. "Excuse me?"

He smiled, almost kindly. "Vanessa once told me that her first love was someone who lived near her grandparents." He looked at her sheepishly. "I can say this now—she tried, but she never got over you."

Makenna kept her face neutral, but her heart was about to beat out of her chest. She didn't know what to say.

Vanessa and Declan walked back into the room, saving her. She and Daniel hopped up from their seats.

"Daniel," Vanessa said, noticing their discomfort. "You can stay here tonight. I'm going to quickly pack a bag and stay with Makenna." She looked over at Makenna and saw her nod. Vanessa could see the surprise just under the surface, but Makenna covered it well. She turned to keep them from seeing her smile and walked down the hall to her bedroom.

In an attempt to ease the intensity in the room Declan asked, "How was the taco place, Coach?"

Makenna chuckled, appreciating what he was trying to do. "It was great. We tried all of them. Their shrimp ones weren't as good as your mom's though."

"I'm not surprised. She is the best cook, or I guess I should say chef."

"Did your coaches give you workouts for the holidays, son? Or do you have practice at the university?" Daniel asked.

"We're doing workouts they gave us until after Christmas and then we're up at the school three times a week. It's not a big deal for me now since Mom came here."

"Yeah, but don't you want to see your friends back home?"

"I'll see them when I come visit you."

Vanessa came back into the room and Makenna released a breath she didn't realize she'd been holding. Vanessa smiled at her and immediately she felt calm.

"Okay boys, I'll leave you to it. Merry Christmas, Daniel. Declan, see you tomorrow."

Makenna got up and turned to Daniel. "It's nice to meet you."

"You too, Makenna. Thanks for all you're doing for Declan." He turned to Vanessa. "Merry Christmas. I hope you get everything you want."

Vanessa tilted her head and smiled at him, then looked at Makenna. "Me too."

They walked out the front door and Vanessa immediately grabbed Makenna's hand and squeezed. She brought it to her lips and kissed the back of it. "You'll never believe what my mother told Daniel. Declan filled me in."

Makenna had mixed emotions. She knew it was a good thing that Vanessa was coming with her, but she was also wary of what her mother had done. And then, all of that was forgotten when she realized that Vanessa was spending the night.

8

They walked into Makenna's house and the cats couldn't be bothered with them. No meows, no cuddles. They barely lifted their heads from the chair and ottoman each were lazily draped over.

"Hmm, guess they didn't miss me," Makenna commented.

Vanessa put her bag on the floor and grabbed Makenna's waist, pulling her close. "I missed you."

Makenna gasped and giggled, putting her arms on Vanessa's shoulders. "I was with you. How could you miss me?"

"I missed this," she said, leaning in and claiming Makenna's lips in a tender kiss.

Makenna moaned and brought her hands to either side of Vanessa's face. She pulled back slightly and looked into Vanessa's eyes, searching for answers.

"Thanks for letting me stay here tonight. I know I kind of forced the situation."

A slow smile tugged at the corners of Makenna's mouth.

"I want to be honest with you, Ken. I wanted to come here tonight to show that I mean what I say. No one and nothing is going to come between us this time." She searched Makenna's eyes and could see the apprehension.

"I believe what you say. I do. But Nessa, you don't know what your mother will do this time."

"Come sit down and let me explain what Declan told me in the kitchen." She took Makenna's hand and led them to the couch. They sat down and Vanessa held Makenna's hand in both of hers.

Makenna looked up at her and smiled, waiting patiently for her to begin.

"My mother told Daniel that I had lost my mind and had run off with my lesbian lover to live where Declan was and ruin his life."

Makenna's eyes widened and she sighed. "Oh my God," she said slowly.

"I know. Dramatic, much?" She chuckled. "I'm glad that Daniel told Declan the truth and didn't try to make something up."

"What did Declan do?"

"He told Daniel what she did to us all those years ago and how we happened to meet again."

"And Daniel?"

"He knew that she had come between me and my first love. He simply assumed it was a boy, not you. At the time it all seemed so hopeless that I didn't correct him and didn't want to talk about it."

"That's why he said that," Makenna mumbled to herself.

"Said what?"

"While you were in the kitchen we were talking a bit about Declan. He looked at me like a light bulb went on in his head. And he said, 'You're the one, aren't you.' He went on to say that you tried, but never got over me."

Vanessa smiled. "It's true. And I won't let that happen again, Makenna. I don't care what she does. You've given us this chance."

Makenna still wondered what Vanessa's mother would do next. "I'm the one that's been out all this time, but your mother kind of scares me."

Vanessa searched her face and then realization hit her. "Oh my

God, Makenna. I see what I'm asking now. Why would you want to be with me when you could be with a woman with a normal family?" She dropped her head and tears stung her eyes.

"Hey," Makenna said, reaching out and gently raising Vanessa's chin with her finger. When she saw the tears her hands went to Vanessa's face. "Do you see me being with a woman who has a normal family? That's not happening." She smiled. "Because I love you, Nessa. You are who I want to be with."

Vanessa sniffed. "This is like a Christmas miracle that I've found you again. I've always loved you. I told you that and it's true."

"I know," Makenna whispered, kissing the corner of her mouth. "I know." She brought their lips together in the most tender kiss. "I've always loved you too."

Vanessa captured Makenna's lips and deepened the kiss, pushing Makenna back on the couch. She sat back up, her chest heaving. "I feel like I'm nineteen again." Then she pulled her sweater over her head and threw it on the floor. Makenna's eyes widened when she saw the red lace bra Vanessa wore and she ran her tongue over her bottom lip, unaware she was doing it. She took Makenna's hands and pulled her back up, doing the same to her sweater.

"Come on, I'm not eighteen anymore. I have a lovely bed waiting for us," Makenna said, getting up and leading them to the bedroom. Over her shoulder she said, "Just so you know, I've never brought anyone else here." They walked into the bedroom and Vanessa spun her around.

"I don't care about before. I want this moment with you." Her hands rested on Makenna's hips like they were meant to be there.

"But Nessa," Makenna said, her hands on Vanessa's back, "I want more. I don't want just this moment. I want them all."

"They're yours. All of me, I'm yours, Kenna." She kissed Makenna, leaving no doubt her intentions and her future.

That's all Makenna needed to hear. She kissed her way down Vanessa's neck and slowly lowered her bra strap. The red lace made her smile as she kissed her way from Vanessa's shoulder across her collarbones to the other side.

As much as Vanessa wanted Makenna, she threw her head back, allowing Makenna to worship her with that glorious mouth. Makenna reached around and unclasped her bra, tossing it aside. Her hands slid around and she cupped Vanessa's full breasts in both hands. "Just as beautiful as I remember," she whispered. "Even more so."

Vanessa reached around and unclasped Makenna's bra, lowering it with the other. Makenna's hands felt heavenly and she closed her eyes in bliss. She felt Makenna's hands at the front of her pants. "Let me," she said breathlessly. They made quick work of the rest of their clothes.

Makenna took her hand and led her around to one side of the bed. She climbed on the bed on her knees and guided Vanessa to do the same. She looked down at their bodies so close together where they belonged and inhaled their scents. She ran her hands up the outside of both of Vanessa's arms and could see her chest rise and fall. The desire in her eyes had turned them a deep mahogany color that burned Makenna's skin wherever they lingered.

"I love you," Makenna whispered. She trailed her lips along her neck and down to her left breast. She licked around her nipple as it hardened and then took it into her mouth. She could feel as well as hear the moan come from Vanessa's chest. Vanessa had her hands in Makenna's hair, holding her somewhat in place. She continued to trail kisses back up her chest and claimed her mouth once again with her lips and tongue, pinching her right nipple.

Vanessa groaned into Makenna's mouth as her hands found Makenna's round full breasts begging to be touched. Her nipples were hard and Vanessa tweaked them both. She ran one hand around to Makenna's back as her other hand leisurely slid down her hip and across her stomach to find her curly hairs.

Their tongues darted and danced inside one another's mouths. Makenna mirrored Vanessa's hand and slid hers down to find her wetness. This first time after twenty-five years had to be synchronous. They wanted to be inside one another at the same time. After all these years their bodies still knew what the other wanted.

Vanessa pulled her lips away slightly. "I love you, Ken," she said against her lips and then entered her with one finger. Makenna's moan was trapped in Vanessa's mouth. Vanessa almost came right then as Makenna entered her.

They each added a finger and pushed deeper inside. Makenna swore that Vanessa touched her heart and then they found their rhythm. Their hearts were attached just like their bodies. They made love with their eyes, their bodies and their souls. Makenna came undone as she looked into her eyes. She could see Vanessa give her heart and soul to her right then. Their eyes filled with tears as Vanessa bit her bottom lip and pulled Makenna closer as the orgasm grabbed her. They stayed like this for a few moments as the waves swept over them again and again.

A smile crept onto Vanessa's face. "My legs are shaking. I've got to lay down."

Makenna smiled back at her. "One, two, three." They both fell over on the bed, arms and legs wrapped around one another. "I've dreamed about this so many times. You're right, this is a Christmas miracle."

"Mmm." Vanessa laid back and took Makenna in her arms, resting her head on her chest.

Makenna raised her head. "Hey, do you want to spend Christmas Eve with me?"

"Really?"

"Yes, really. Declan's going to be at Daniel's. I'd love for you to spend it with me and my family."

"What do you think they're going to say?"

"Does it matter?"

"It matters. Don't they know I'm the girl that broke your heart?"

"But you're here now."

"And I'm not leaving you ever again."

Makenna smiled. It felt so good to hear those words, but she wasn't a kid anymore and knew that life could always get in the way.

"I'd love to spend Christmas with you and every day after. But right now, I'm going to love on you all night long."

"Mmm," Makenna said as Vanessa pushed her onto her back and straddled her. She whipped her auburn curls back and Makenna felt the years fall away.

9

M akenna and Vanessa lay languidly in one another's arms. The sun peeked through the window past the blinds.

"I could do this all day," Vanessa said, stroking her hand up and down Makenna's back. She felt Makenna smile against her chest. "Did you have plans for today?"

"You know," she said, propping up on her elbow looking mischievously into Vanessa's eyes. "I have no idea. I think it was two days ago when this whirlwind stormed back into my life and everything changed."

Vanessa softly smiled and caressed the side of Makenna's face. "Two days, huh. A lot can happen in two days."

"A broken heart can be put back together."

Vanessa's smile grew. "It can."

"Don't you have plans? Declan leaves in a couple of days."

"He does, but we didn't plan anything."

"I was going on a hike today, but I could do that some other time."

"A hike? That sounds fun. Declan could go with us."

"I thought you wanted to do this all day." Makenna leaned in and kissed her.

"Mmm," Vanessa moaned. "I do."

"We could always spend the day in bed after he leaves," Makenna said, nuzzling Vanessa's neck.

"You keep doing that and we won't be going anywhere anytime soon." Vanessa moved her head to give Makenna better access.

After a few moments Makenna pulled back. "Okay," she said, sighing. "Text him and see if he'd like to go on the Burma trail with us. He'll know it from his workouts. They sometimes run there. There's something I'd like to show you."

Vanessa reached over and grabbed her phone from the night stand. She sent the text and waited for Declan to reply. "What do you want to show me?" she asked, turning her attention back to her love.

"It's kind of a surprise. I'll explain when we get there."

Vanessa's phone pinged with Declan's reply. "He's in. What time?'

"We've got to wait for it to warm up a bit. Tell him we'll come get him in two hours."

Vanessa sent the text and immediately got a thumbs up from her son. She put her phone back on the table and rolled on top of Makenna. "We've got two hours, let's make the most of it." Her eyebrows wiggled up and down.

Makenna giggled. "We have to shower and eat something before we go, Nessa."

"We will. I know exactly what I want." She slid down Makenna's body and found what she craved.

* * *

Makenna parked in the almost empty lot at the trailhead. They each had a bottle of water and were dressed in layers. Declan left his jacket in the car because he planned to run the trail.

"Where do you plan to go, Coach?" Declan asked, stretching before he took off.

"We're going left at the first fork. About a mile from here there's something I want to show your mom."

"Sounds good. I'll go right and make the loop back up to you. I'll have my phone even though reception sucks in some places."

"Okay, we'll see you in a little while then."

"Have fun and be careful, Dec," Vanessa said, not able to keep her motherly instinct quiet.

He smiled. "I will, Mom. Have fun. Makenna will take good care of you."

Vanessa nodded then smiled at Makenna. "I know she will." She boldly took Makenna's hand as they walked down the trail.

Declan watched them for a moment, smiling at the casual gesture. He didn't know if he'd ever seen his mom this happy and hoped it stayed that way.

"Are you cold?" Makenna asked as Vanessa walked next to her.

"No babe, you always warm me up," she said, winking.

Makenna liked the term of endearment she hadn't heard from her in years.

"Just ahead there's a little break in the trees and a gorgeous view of the valley."

"I have a gorgeous view anytime I'm looking at you."

Makenna laughed.

"I'm not trying to be funny. I'm being honest and I'm telling you every day from here on out."

Makenna grabbed her around the waist and pulled her in close so they were face to face. "Thank you, babe," she said, enunciating the last word firmly. "I love the sweet things you say to me and especially love the way you look at me. I always know I'm loved whenever I look into your eyes."

Vanessa visibly softened. She leaned in and brought their lips together. They were cold and firm at first, but quickly thawed and warmed at the contact. "I could kiss you forever," she murmured.

"Mmm, I hope you will."

Vanessa giggled. "We've got it bad."

Makenna joined her. "Yeah we do. Come on, I really do want to show you something."

"Why did we not do this before?" Vanessa asked, following Makenna down the trail.

"It wasn't here. About twenty years ago they started building trails and now it's a wonderful area for hikers and they even have mountain bike trails a little farther over."

They reached the overlook and Vanessa took a couple of pictures with them arm in arm and the valley as a backdrop.

They continued on, taking the left fork and it wasn't long until she guided them down a little patch just off the trail.

"I come here a lot," Makenna began. "I've poured out my wishes and hopes and dreams in this spot. I always felt like it was a little magical and now I believe it is." She took Vanessa's hand and nodded with her head. "Look! What do you see?"

Vanessa scanned the trees, unsure at first and then she saw it. She squeezed Makenna's hand. "Oh Ken, I see us." In front of her were two trees that had started with their trunks side by side. But over the years one had begun to slant toward the other, then it straightened and grew up. At the same time the other tree began to lean toward its mate then grew up and around the other. The trees formed a loose spiral around one another at the trunk and then their limbs were entwined together further up. She'd never seen anything like it. They looked like lovers in a hug, wrapping themselves around the other.

"I found them several years ago right after my ex told me I wouldn't give myself completely to anyone else. I knew she was right. I happened upon these trees and felt the strangest energy. It felt like they were welcoming me, asking me to stay." She walked over and ran her hand along one of the trees.

Vanessa mirrored her movement on the other one.

"I come here to think and end up daydreaming about you almost every time. It was oddly comforting in a way. It sounds foolish, but I imagined you here with me someday."

"Oh wow," Vanessa said reverently. "That's not foolish. It sounds magical. Like the Christmas miracle I talked about last night."

She put her arm around Makenna and laid her head on her shoulder. "Thank you for bringing me here. It feels so peaceful."

"It does." Makenna put both her arms around Vanessa and pulled her into a hug just like the trees. Vanessa knew right then this would become an important place to them.

"Hey," Declan called to them, out of breath. He walked up and stopped to take a drink from his water bottle. "Would you look at that! Those trees grew around one another."

"I know. Isn't it remarkable!" Vanessa said, her eyes sparkling. "Would you take a picture of us with them?" She handed her phone to Declan.

"Sure." He stepped back a few paces and waited for them to pose.

They turned toward him. Vanessa had her arm around Makenna's shoulders since she was slightly taller. The smiles on their faces rivaled the sun.

"I don't mean to embarrass you, Declan, but I'm going to kiss Makenna and want you to take the picture."

He chuckled. "It's okay, Mom."

Makenna could feel the top of her ears turning red with Vanessa's statement and Declan's reply.

"It's okay, Coach. Really."

Vanessa placed her hands on Makenna's hips as Makenna's hands rested on her upper arms. Vanessa smiled and looked into the most beautiful golden brown eyes that had turned radiant as the sun. She whispered, "I love you, babe." Then she leaned in and their lips touched.

Makenna felt a spark of energy fly from Vanessa's lips through her body and land in her heart. The cracks that had been there all those years, the very ones that had begun to heal the last two days, were suddenly gone. Her heart was whole again. The scars faded away and it pumped vigorously for Vanessa.

"Got it!" Declan exclaimed.

They pulled apart and Makenna's eyes were wide with wonder. When she looked at Vanessa she knew she'd felt it too. Those darkened amber eyes twinkled like the Christmas miracle she'd alluded to earlier. This place really was magical.

"Aww, they're good," Declan said, looking at the pictures he took.

"See!" He handed the phone back to his mom. "Are you done or were you going to keep hiking?"

Makenna looked over Vanessa's shoulder at the photos. "Nope, we're done. Do you want to run to the car or walk with us?"

"I'll run."

"Here," Makenna said, fishing the keys out of her pocket. "We'll be there in a bit."

"Okay. You kids behave now," he said playfully and ran off.

They both laughed.

"These pictures are great. I'll text them to you," Vanessa said, smiling at her phone.

"I love you, Nessa."

She put her phone down and looked at Makenna, a little surprised at her serious tone.

Makenna had tears in her eyes, "Thank you for coming back and finding me."

"Oh baby," Vanessa said, pulling Makenna into her arms. "I'll never leave you again." She held her tighter and buried her nose in Makenna's hair, inhaling the sweet fragrance of the future.

10

Declan was scrolling on his phone when they made it back to the car. Vanessa smiled to herself, thrilled at what a wonderful day this was. She was with her two favorite people and she and Makenna had a real shot at a life together.

They got in the car and Vanessa looked back at her son, his nose buried in his phone. "Let's talk about plans."

Declan looked up at her warily and put his phone down. "Okay," he said, unsure of what direction this conversation was taking.

"It's four days until Christmas. Are you going to your dad's on Christmas Eve?"

"I think I'm going to go on the 23rd. I don't have to worry about you being by yourself and I wouldn't mind catching up with Lacey and Kyle."

Makenna looked in the rear view mirror and smiled at Declan. He saw her smile and returned it with a thumbs up. She shook her head and laughed.

"You know you don't have to worry about me being alone."

"I know, Mom. But sometimes I do."

"Well, do you have plans today?"

"Not really, what did you have in mind?"

"I told Kenna that we like to watch movies together and we're serious about snacks."

Declan smiled at the shortened form of Makenna's name that his mom sometimes used. "We are *very* serious about snacks. Would you like to go home and watch a movie? I wasn't planning to go out until later."

"How about this. I'll get the snacks together and you and Makenna choose the movie."

"Sounds good to me."

"I'm in, but I need to stop at home and let the cats in," Makenna said, steering the car toward her house.

When Makenna pulled in, both cats came running.

"Can I meet them?" Declan asked.

"Of course. Come on in."

They all walked in as the cats sang their familiar song. Once again Makenna was surprised when Max came to Vanessa and then wove through Declan's legs too.

"Let me put food out for them. I'll just be a minute. Nessa, feel free to show Declan around."

She took care of the cats as Vanessa and Declan walked into the living room.

"This is a great place, Coach. It fits you."

"Thanks."

"Um," Vanessa stammered, walking over to Makenna. She quietly asked, "Would you want to pack a bag and stay with me tonight?"

Makenna's eyes widened and Declan chuckled at their discomfort.

"It's okay, you're both adults."

"I know that," Vanessa said, exasperated. "But I've never had anyone over before. Would you rather we stay over here? Why is this so awkward?"

He threw his head back and laughed. "No, it's fine. I don't mind where you stay as long as you're together. It's obvious you want to be."

Makenna didn't think she could turn any redder; she put her face in her hands and started to laugh too. If anyone would have told her last week she would be staying the night with her long lost first love and favorite student athlete, she would've laughed hysterically. Yet, here she was: in her living room with her long lost first love and her favorite student athlete, deciding where to stay the night.

Vanessa looked from Declan to Makenna and couldn't stop the laughter bubbling from her chest.

"I'll be right back," Makenna said, going to her bedroom.

Vanessa looked over at Declan. "Are you sure you're okay with this?"

He sighed. "Yeah Mom. Don't you think it's your turn to be happy? Coach Markus is the best."

Vanessa smiled, looking down the hall. "She is, isn't she?"

* * *

"Here come the snacks," Vanessa said, walking in with bowls of popcorn and setting them on the coffee table. "Declan, get our butterscotch treats and I'll grab the drinks."

"I can help." Makenna jumped up and followed her into the kitchen.

"Grab those Milk Duds and Sour Patch Kids, babe," she said to Makenna as she carried the drinks out on a tray.

"You keep Milk Duds and Sour Patch Kids in the pantry?"

"Doesn't everyone?" Vanessa asked, looking over her shoulder.

Makenna had a surprised look on her face. Vanessa started laughing. "I'm kidding. I like Milk Duds and Declan likes Sour Patch Kids for our movie nights. I picked some up the other day."

"I'm happy to share mine with you, Coach."

"You know I will, too." Vanessa winked.

"You *are* serious about snacks. What is this?" Makenna asked, looking into a bowl Vanessa handed her.

"This is a treat that Mom and I created years ago and we always have it when we watch movies. It's cashew pieces with butterscotch chips. Mom melts the chips on the nuts in the microwave and then you stir it up. It's delicious!"

Skeptical, Makenna looked down into her bowl.

"Here," Vanessa said, handing her a spoon. "You'll need this. It really is good. Try it."

Makenna took her spoon and dug into the creamy and chunky mixture. She took half a spoonful and put it into her mouth. Her eyes lit up and Vanessa and Declan both started nodding.

"Mmm, you're right, this is so good," she said between bites.

"It's one of my favorites." Declan plopped down in the chair and grabbed the remote.

"Why would you need other snacks if you have this!" Makenna exclaimed around another bite.

Vanessa smiled, obviously pleased Makenna liked it. "You can't eat a lot of it. You'll see. I've also made two kinds of popcorn."

"Two kinds?"

"Yeah. I like to add surprises to mine like pretzels or candy," Declan said, reaching for a bowl.

"And I like to melt and drizzle white chocolate over mine, then throw in some chow mein noodles."

"Wow, you two are really creative!" Makenna marveled.

Declan laughed. "We like to experiment, don't we Mom?"

Vanessa smiled between bites. "That we do. What movie did you decide on?"

"*Krampus*," replied Declan.

Vanessa swung her head around to look at Makenna next to her on the couch. "Did you let him talk you into a horror movie? He loves them and I tolerate them. I didn't think you liked them."

"Well," she answered, shrugging.

"We can watch something else," Vanessa said, grabbing a blanket from the end of the couch.

"Mom will take care of you, Coach. You don't have to be scared." Declan scanned the TV as he searched for the movie.

Vanessa looked over at Makenna and scooted up next to her. "He's right. I won't let anything happen to you." She put her arm around Makenna and whispered in her ear, "I'll kiss you during the scary parts. That's better than covering your eyes."

Makenna giggled.

"The movie hasn't even started yet!" Declan teased. "Kids," he mumbled.

They quieted down as Declan pressed play. All three of them were engrossed in the movie, busy munching on their snacks.

After a while, during one particular scene Vanessa shouted, "Don't go in there!"

"Nope, he's going in," murmured Declan.

The scene continued to get scarier and Vanessa leaned in and whispered to Makenna, "I'd better cover your eyes." She reached up gently and placed her hand across her eyes. When she uncovered them a horrible looking creature jumped out and attacked the two people in the forest.

Makenna screamed and Vanessa and Declan started to laugh. "You did that on purpose!" she said, feigning anger.

Vanessa grabbed her face between her hands. "I'm sorry, baby. I didn't mean to."

"I think you did," she whispered, not wanting to disrupt the movie.

"Maybe just a little," she said quietly, crinkling her eyes. "I'm sorry." She leaned in and grazed her lips against Makenna's. She pulled back with fire in her eyes and brought their lips together again with purpose. Her heart immediately sped up and her breath quickened. Just like that, Makenna lit her body on fire.

Makenna pulled back and shook her head. "Oh no you don't," she whispered softly. "That's what you get for scaring me."

Vanessa narrowed her eyes and then smiled, defeated. She leaned back, took Makenna's hand in hers and imagined what they'd do after Declan went out.

They behaved through the rest of the movie. Near the end they breathed a sigh of relief.

"Oh, he was just dreaming," said Makenna.

"Wait for it," Declan commented, his eyes never leaving the screen.

And then the surprise ending came on the screen.

"Oh no!" Makenna shouted.

"I did not see that coming!" exclaimed Vanessa.

"Told you," Declan said, pleased.

The credits came on and they all moved around reaching for popcorn.

"That wasn't too scary was it, Coach?"

"I just made it through. You don't watch horror movies all the time, do you? Is this a test I have to pass or something I have to get used to?"

"Of course not," Vanessa said, standing up. "A test, huh? You think Declan and I are testing you?"

"I wouldn't put it past either one of you."

Declan laughed.

"I know she knows me, but I'd say she's come to know you pretty well too, D." Vanessa grinned.

"Oh, she knows me, sometimes better than I know me," he said, getting up and taking his bowls to the kitchen.

Makenna followed Vanessa into the kitchen with her bowls and set them in the sink.

"Thanks for letting me hang out with you today; it was fun," Declan said, leaning against the cabinet.

"It *was* fun," Vanessa agreed, thinking how easy it felt with the three of them together.

"It should be me thanking you two for including me in your family movie time," Makenna said, rinsing out the bowls.

"I don't think so, Coach. You're family, too."

Makenna's heart swelled in her chest at Declan's words. "Thanks Declan."

He grinned and walked out of the kitchen, down the hall to his room.

Vanessa came over to Makenna, turned off the water and took her in her arms. She leaned in and brought their lips together to finish the kiss she'd started earlier. Her tongue ran across Makenna's bottom lip, awaiting access. She felt Makenna soften and her lips open. Vanessa searched and found Makenna's tongue and lost her breath. This was home, her arms wrapped around the woman that kept her heart. Their souls, bodies, and love intertwined just like the trees she'd seen earlier today.

She pulled back slightly, not wanting the moment to end, and whispered into Makenna's ear, "I love you so much. Just let me hold you."

Makenna answered by pulling her closer and burying her nose in her hair, breathing in the cherry almond scent of her shampoo from their shower together earlier. She could feel their hearts beating together as if there was no space between them.

They could hear Declan walking down the hall and pulled apart slowly, smiling at one another, their hearts doing the talking, no words needed.

"I'm going to head out. I have my key to the back door, Mom."

"Have fun," she said, refraining from sharing any motherly guidance she wanted to give.

He stopped at the door and turned around. "That's it? Have fun?"

"That's it," she said, looking at Makenna then back at Declan.

"Hmm, you must want to get rid of me."

Vanessa laughed and held up her hands. "I can't win with you. First, you roll your eyes if I say anything and now you stop because I didn't."

He pointed from one to the other. "*You* have fun," he said, emphasizing the first word.

"Oh we will," Makenna assured him.

Showing surprise, he walked out the door.

"You've got to knock him down a few rungs every now and then," she said, nodding at Vanessa with spunk.

"Well done," Vanessa complimented with admiration.

"He doesn't have a chance between the two of us."

Vanessa liked this side of Makenna. "We do make a good team."

"The best," Makenna mumbled, looking at Vanessa's lips then snaking her hand behind Vanessa's neck, pulling her into a greedy kiss. Makenna took her lips and ravaged them with her own. Sometimes she couldn't resist the pull of Vanessa. She didn't even know she was doing it, but she could ignite a fire in Makenna that could only be satiated with her lips or her touch. It was like that twenty-five years ago and remained still.

When Makenna pulled back to breathe Vanessa instantly missed her lips. Her eyes flew open to see the deep dark hunger in her lover's eyes. Vanessa didn't say a word. She took Makenna's hand and led her down the hall into her old bedroom.

As she closed the door there was a reverent silence along with a youthful yearning to love and explore one another that lingered from the past. They slowly undressed together, the room dimly lit with street lights creeping in through the narrow slits in the drapes. Vanessa could barely make out Makenna's face, but she saw that smile that was only for her. Then they faced one another, naked, their hearts wide open. Their love there for the other to see, no doubts, no fears. Just love. Desire, trust and pure love one for the other.

Vanessa held out her hand and Makenna took it. She backed up toward the bed until she could feel it against her legs. She turned them around and placed her hands on the outside of Makenna's arms and gently pushed her down on the bed until she was sitting.

She looked down into those beautiful brown eyes, her hair fanned out over her shoulders. Then she lowered herself down so she was on her knees between Makenna's legs. She ran her hands from Makenna's knees up her thighs and around, her fingers tickling the top of her backside. She spread her fingers out and pulled Makenna toward her until she felt Makenna's wet center against her stomach. She closed her eyes, committing this warm feeling and enticing aroma to memory.

She could hear as well as feel their ragged breaths. It was like the melody of their love playing out in stereo. Their hearts were woven together, orchestrating every move in a dance to bring ultimate pleasure to their bodies. And as their pleasure grew their souls were mingling together, fusing to become one.

"I'm yours. All of me," Vanessa whispered.

"Take me, Nessa. Make me yours," Makenna replied breathlessly.

Their lips came together gently at first and as their hunger grew their passion followed. It was their lips' turn to dance to the music of their love.

They were both panting when Vanessa began to kiss her way down to Makenna's breasts. She circled her nipple and then flattened her tongue against it as she pulled Makenna closer. Then she sucked the hardened bud into her mouth and Makenna threw her head back, her hands buried in Vanessa's hair.

"Oh God, Nessa."

When Vanessa heard this a smile tickled the corners of her mouth and she bit down. Makenna moaned and Vanessa felt her wetness intensify between her own legs. She began to push Makenna's hips back on the bed and Makenna put her hands behind her, propping up. She looked down at Vanessa and saw a wicked smile and fire in her eyes.

Vanessa's hands came around to Makenna's thighs and she looked down at Makenna's wetness. Good God, the beauty. She dropped her head down and licked slowly across Makenna's stomach, enjoying every sensation and taste. When she couldn't wait any longer she pushed on Makenna's thighs, spreading her legs wider. She took a moment and inhaled the sweet and sharp scent that was her Makenna. Because that's what she was, all hers, and Vanessa was Makenna's and no one else's. It wasn't a matter of possessiveness or control, it just was. They were made for each other, to be as one.

She opened her eyes and leaned in for a lick. Her tongue went in and out and between the soft folds of Makenna's goodness. She circled the bundle of lust that pulsed against her tongue. Makenna's breathing and moaning got louder.

"Nessa," she whispered over and over. "I love you."

Vanessa wasn't trying to tease her, but she was enjoying this so much. Her tongue circled around Makenna's opening and she felt her fall on her back, her hands clutching the quilt on the bed.

"Oh yes, baby, yes," Makenna hummed between a moan and a groan.

Vanessa pushed her tongue inside and pulled Makenna's hips

toward her. She licked up all of her delicious wetness and then sucked her clit deeply inside her mouth.

Makenna arched her back and sat up, grabbing her knees and planting her heels on the edge of the bed.

Vanessa slid two fingers inside Makenna and continued to suck her clit. She would never tire of how it felt to be inside this woman. Her heart was so full and then she felt Makenna's hands on her head pulling her up.

"I've got to have you here, babe. Now," she said, pulling Vanessa's wet lips to hers. Their lips met in an explosion of sensations and taste. Vanessa thought she'd just tasted Makenna's best flavor, but this was a whole new level of deliciousness. Their tongues stroked and licked and twirled.

Vanessa felt Makenna's walls begin to tighten around her fingers and she pushed a little deeper and curled them up to find Makenna's favorite velvety spot. Makenna's arms tightened around Vanessa and her cry was swallowed into the bosom of this exquisite kiss.

Vanessa kept her hand buried as the after effects continued to roll through Makenna. Finally, Makenna's hand rested on Vanessa's and she gently removed it. Vanessa propped her head up on her hand and smiled down at Makenna. The look of bliss on her face was almost too much. She could feel tears prick the back of her eyes.

"I have never felt so close to you, so worshipped by you, so loved by you," Makenna said, rubbing her hand over Vanessa's hair, looking into her eyes with respect, adoration, and love.

"You've got all of me, Ken."

"And I'm yours."

11

Makenna stirred when she felt the hand around her middle begin to pull away. She grabbed it and kissed the back of it before tucking it between her breasts. She heard a chuckle behind her and rolled over, still holding Vanessa's hand.

"Good morning," Vanessa whispered, kissing the back of Makenna's hand.

"Good morning." Makenna smiled sleepily. "These lips need your lips," she mumbled, pointing from her lips to Vanessa's.

Vanessa leaned in and kissed her.

"Mmm, much better," Makenna mumbled, her eyes closed.

"You are so adorable in the mornings. My sleepyhead hasn't changed," Vanessa said.

Makenna could feel and hear the smile in her voice. When she opened her eyes she wasn't disappointed. Vanessa's natural beauty was on full display, especially in the morning. Her curly hair was mussed, her eyes were bright, and her face glowed with love. Makenna couldn't believe the desire that quickly built in her chest and moved down to her center. "You are so beautiful," she whispered adoringly.

"Right!" Vanessa responded, her eyes twinkling. "I know just how beautiful all this must look," she said, circling a finger around her face.

"You are," Makenna said, rolling close so her body was halfway on Vanessa's.

"Don't start something you don't intend to finish," Vanessa warned.

Makenna raised her eyebrows then remembered where they were and realized Declan was right down the hall.

"You don't have to stop," Vanessa said, running her hand through Makenna's hair.

"Maybe we shouldn't."

"Why not?" Vanessa asked.

"Because he's just down the hall."

"That never bothered you when it was my grandparents."

Makenna's eyes grew big, then she thought about it. "That was different."

"How so? Are you saying whenever Declan is staying with us we're not going to have sex?"

"I don't know what I'm saying. This is all new!" Makenna said, exasperated.

Vanessa smiled and pulled Makenna's face down into a kiss. "He knows what we did at your house when I spent the night and he knows what we did here last night, too."

Makenna's face softened. "Last night," she said dreamily.

"Yeah, last night was..." Vanessa struggled to find the words.

"Exactly."

Vanessa suddenly pushed Makenna onto her back and straddled her. "How about we go make breakfast and talk about all the changes we need to make to the house?"

"That's a good idea."

"But first," Vanessa said seriously. "Would you go out with me tonight?"

"Yes," Makenna said, drawing the word out. "But wait, it's Declan's last night here."

"I know. I've already talked to him about it. I want to take you to that Christmas Stroll we did all those years ago."

"Yeah? I'd like that."

"And this time, the end of the date will be much different."

"I can't wait."

Vanessa stared down into Makenna's happy face knowing she had put that joy there. She grabbed her hands, pinning them beside her head, and slowly lowered her lips down to Makenna's. Their lips met and a charge shot through Vanessa's body. Her tongue slid in, bathing Makenna's mouth in love. She felt Makenna's fingers tighten around hers and gently ended the kiss.

She pulled back to see Makenna, quirking an eyebrow. "Now who's starting something?"

"Sometimes you take my breath away and I simply have to kiss you."

Makenna gave her an affirming smile. "I know, baby." She started to sit up. "As much as I like you on top of me, I also like food. Let's go make breakfast."

"Okay," Vanessa said softly. "We'll continue this later."

Ten minutes later, Makenna was carrying out Vanessa's instructions since she was the chef, but she was also in thought. She couldn't help but replay the last few days in her head. She and Vanessa had quickly taken up where they'd left off after the truth came out. Even with all of Vanessa's assurances that nothing and no one would ever come between them again, Makenna still had an uneasy feeling at times. This didn't make sense because she had never been this happy and she had never felt closer to Vanessa than she had last night. She believed in her heart that she and Vanessa were meant to live this life together. Her apprehension must be residual from the past and Vanessa's mother's evil manipulations.

"Babe?" Vanessa asked.

Makenna was still in thought.

"Baby?" Vanessa prompted again as she concentrated on whisking the eggs.

Worried about Makenna's silence, Vanessa finally looked up. She leaned over and put her hand over Makenna's which was busy peeling an orange. "Hey, you okay?" she asked softly.

Makenna looked up, surprised. "Yeah, why?"

"I called you and you didn't hear me. What were you thinking about? Your face was very serious."

"Nothing to worry about."

"Don't do that. Please. Tell me, I know something's wrong."

Makenna sighed. "Really, it's nothing. I was thinking about the last few days."

"And?" Vanessa stopped what she was doing. Suddenly her stomach was filled with butterflies. She turned Makenna towards her.

"I was thinking how I've never been this happy. And I know in my heart that we're supposed to live this life together." She wiped her hands and put them on Vanessa's shoulders. She could feel the tension in them ease with her touch.

Vanessa released the breath she'd been holding. "Then why did you look so serious? You scared me."

Makenna smiled. "I'm sorry. Sometimes I still feel a little uneasy."

"Uneasy? About what?"

"About something coming between us. We haven't had the best luck."

"I've told you. Nothing and no one—"

Makenna put two fingers over Vanessa's lips to stop her. "I know you have. I believe you. I believe in us. But sometimes don't you wish everyone could just be happy for us and not have to have an opinion?"

Vanessa smiled and curled a strand of hair behind Makenna's ear. "As far as I'm concerned the only person who matters has given us his blessing, wouldn't you agree?"

Makenna smiled back at her. "I do."

"I hope that your family will be accepting of us, but if they're not then we'll deal with it. Together."

"But what about your mother?"

"It doesn't matter, Ken. She won't accept us and I'm okay with that. I'm living my life for the happiness of you and Declan and me. We have so much living to do. So many more moments to share."

"We do. Like tonight."

"That's right, I'm looking forward to that stroll with my Christmas miracle, hand in hand. But right now, I'm hungry. How about you?"

"I am," she said, leaning in and caressing Vanessa's lips with her own. Vanessa had eased her doubts by being realistic that not everyone would be happy for them. But they could handle anything together. And she was sure that that's what they would be from now on—together.

Vanessa pulled back, desire smoldering in her eyes. "Maybe breakfast can wait." She was about to lean in for another kiss when they heard Declan's door open. She leaned her forehead against Makenna's and smiled. They went back to their preparations as Declan walked into the kitchen.

"Good morning. Want to join us for breakfast?"

"Morning. Sure. I smell coffee." He walked over to the coffee maker and poured a cup.

"How was your night?"

"It was good. Played video games and watched a movie. What did you two get up to?" he asked, looking at his phone.

Vanessa and Makenna looked at one another. "Oh, not much," Makenna said, winking at Vanessa.

"Uh-huh, I'm sure you found something to do," he said, still scrolling on his phone.

"Omelets coming up," Vanessa said. "Hope everyone's hungry."

Just as they had that first night together, they gathered around the table and had breakfast as a family. Declan entertained them with stories of his friends. Makenna's uneasiness was gone. And Vanessa soaked in this wondrous moment, thankful for what she knew was a Christmas miracle.

* * *

After cleaning up the kitchen together, Makenna turned to Vanessa. "What's the plan for this stroll down memory lane tonight?"

"Well, if I remember correctly and I know I do because this night has been burned into my brain for twenty-five tormenting years, you picked me up. So, do you mind driving tonight?"

"I do not mind at all. What time do you want me to pick you up?"

"What do you mean? Are you going somewhere?"

Makenna chuckled. "As much as I love spending every minute with you—" She walked over and kissed Vanessa quickly to temper her next statement. "I have a few things to do today and I would like to look nice for our date tonight."

Vanessa furrowed her brow, obviously in thought as she looked into Makenna's eyes. "We were going to stay at your house that night, so I'm packing a bag and not forgetting it this time."

"Okay." Makenna grinned. "Good plan."

Vanessa wrapped her arms around Makenna and pulled her in close. "I want you to think about something and maybe we can talk about it tonight."

"Okay..." Makenna said suspiciously, putting her hands on Vanessa's shoulders.

"I don't want to spend another night away from you. Ever." Vanessa peered into Makenna's eyes, trying to read her thoughts.

A slow smile crept onto her face. "I'd love for us to find a way to make that happen."

Vanessa returned her smile. "Okay then."

"But you've got to let me go for a little while." Makenna didn't make any move to leave, keeping her hands on Vanessa's shoulders.

Vanessa continued to look into Makenna's eyes. At times it felt like a dream that they had found one another again.

"What?" Makenna asked.

"I love you. That's what."

"I love you, too, Nessa." She leaned in and firmly placed her lips on Vanessa's. "Mmm. Do you realize how hard you are to leave sometimes?"

"Then don't," she said, tilting her head.

Makenna looked down and released a breath. "I'll be back at 6:00 to pick you up."

Vanessa acquiesced with a nod. "See you then." She pecked Makenna's lips and dropped her hands.

Makenna got her bag and headed home. She was nervous and excited about tonight much like she was twenty-five years ago when they'd planned the original date. Maybe she could do something romantic for them to come home to this time.

Tina and Max were happy to see her, but also ready to go outside. She did a little cleaning and went through her mail. It had only been four days since she'd laid eyes on Vanessa again, but it felt like much longer since she'd last been home.

For so many years she'd wondered what their life would have been like. And now she was a little afraid to imagine it. She had no doubts that Vanessa loved her and wanted to be with her, live together and build a life together. But were they really strong enough to withstand what her mother would throw at them? Because they both knew she would. Were they being naive like they had been before, so many years ago?

Makenna walked into her bedroom and looked around. All those questions were flying around her head. Her eyes landed on the bed and she immediately remembered their lovemaking two nights ago. She took a deep breath and closed her eyes, remembering last night in Vanessa's old room at her grandparents' house. It wasn't just Vanessa's touch that Makenna could feel; it was how their hearts talked to one another. It was how their souls were entwined just like those trees. She opened her eyes and knew. A smile crept onto her face and widened as her strength grew. Vanessa kept saying she wouldn't let anything or anyone come between them, but something was missing.

It was her! Makenna believed in them, but she'd let Vanessa shoulder the burden of her mother alone. Not anymore. Right then and there she realized that it was also up to her not to let anyone come between them. If they worked together, no one could. She planned to make sure Vanessa knew that tonight. Again, she looked around the room and knew what she needed to do.

12

Makenna looked at the clock on her dash as she pulled into Vanessa's driveway. Six o'clock on the dot. She breathed a sigh of relief because she'd thought she was going to be late. A grin split her face as she thought back to her hurried preparations for their return to her house later that night. She hoped to show Vanessa just how much she adored her, but also how she cherished their relationship and that she'd do whatever it took for them to thrive.

When she walked up to the front door it swung open before she could knock. Vanessa leapt into her arms and pulled her close. She could feel Vanessa bury her face into her hair and she did the same. Her hair was soft and smelled divine. Makenna couldn't help but moan.

She pulled back slightly. "What a welcome," she said, grinning from ear to ear.

"You were gone too long. I need those lips," Vanessa said, coming in for a kiss. What started with both of them smiling, ready for a sweet kiss, quickly turned into a searing, delicious, passionate kiss that left them both breathless.

When Makenna could speak, her voice was hoarse. "Damn Nessa, I may have to stay away if that's how you kiss me when I get back."

"Don't you dare. There's plenty more where that came from," she replied, winking. "Why were you gone so long? What have you been doing?"

Makenna smiled. "Maybe you're not the only one who wants this night to be special."

Vanessa searched her eyes for a hint but decided she liked the idea of a surprise. "Should we skip the stroll?"

Makenna cocked an eyebrow, but didn't say anything for a moment. "That is a very tempting offer, but I'm looking forward to strolling along hand in hand with the most beautiful woman in the world."

Vanessa dipped her head, suddenly a bit shy. Her heart was so full of love and new beginnings and happiness that she almost couldn't breathe.

"Are you going to let Coach come in, Mom?" Declan called from inside the house.

Vanessa winked and led them into the house, shutting the door behind them.

"Hey Declan. How's it going?" Makenna asked as she walked into the living room to find him scrolling through Netflix. "Big night planned?" she teased, nodding toward the TV.

He narrowed his eyes at her. "Not near as big as yours," he said, teasing right back.

She laughed and was surprised to see Vanessa's cheeks redden at the comment.

"I may hang around here since I have the house to myself."

"Will I see you tomorrow before you leave for your dad's?" Makenna asked, walking over in front of him.

"Probably. I'm not leaving until the afternoon." He looked up and smiled at her. "Why? Do you have a present for me?"

"I don't know, do you have one for me?"

He smiled again. "Maybe."

Vanessa watched this exchange and loved how easy they were with one another. It almost felt like they'd been a family for years.

"Call or text if you need me, Declan," Vanessa said, slipping into her coat.

"I will, Mom. You two have fun. I'm not trying to be a smart ass this time either. I hope this is a magical night like it should have been before."

Makenna patted him on the shoulder as she walked to the door. "Thanks."

They walked out to the car, immediately clasping hands. Makenna smiled to herself and realized she was a bit nervous. She was reminded of the same feeling twenty-five years ago. This time they were going back to her house where they'd be alone, so it was already better. She opened the door for Vanessa and waited for her to get in before shutting it. She ran around to her side and got in.

She let out a deep breath and looked over at Vanessa. "Why do I suddenly feel like I did twenty-five years ago?"

"Because it was a special night, just like this one." Vanessa reached over and cupped one side of Makenna's face. "Don't be nervous, babe. It's just me."

Makenna swallowed and couldn't believe tears sprang to her eyes. "But you're everything, Vanessa." She leaned in and their lips met. That was all Makenna needed to calm her jitters.

She pulled back and started the car. Vanessa held her hand the entire way and they talked about nothing and everything. When they arrived, they got out of the car and began to walk down the street where all the store fronts were brightly decorated. The smells of Christmas wrapped around them like ribbons on a present.

As promised they walked hand in hand and meandered from shop to shop. The Christmas music followed them along the street just like before. They both had a moment of déjà vu.

In one shop there was a display of snow globes. Makenna found one that depicted a jogger running through the forest. It reminded her of Declan when he came with them on their hike.

"I'm going to get this for Declan and surprise him with a Christmas gift after all." She shook it and showed it to Vanessa.

She laughed. "He'll love it."

They continued over to a display with Christmas ornaments.

"Babe, look," Vanessa whispered in awe.

Makenna followed her eyes to an ornament that showed two women hand in hand walking on a snow covered street. She gasped. "I love it!"

"Let's get it. It will be our first ornament together on our first tree."

Makenna nodded her head animatedly, her eyes bright with pure joy.

They made their purchases and continued down the street once again hand in hand. At the next stop they had warm cups of cider. They both giggled as the steam from the cider wound up around their faces and made their eyes water.

After finishing the cider, they strolled up the street, enjoying the Christmas music playing in the background. It was like they were walking in a Christmas card. Vanessa looked ahead and recognized the group of trees where she'd pulled Makenna away from the crowd to steal a kiss.

She grabbed Makenna again and pulled her behind a tree that was much bigger now. "Do you remember this?"

"Of course I do. You told me I'd always be your girl." Makenna's eyes shone with delight.

Vanessa's playful look turned serious. "You always have been, Kenna. I love you so very much." She kissed Makenna's lips just as she had twenty-five years ago. She could feel their hearts beating furiously as they stood chest to chest.

Makenna's arms tightened around Vanessa's neck, holding her lips in place. Their tongues touched and Makenna lost her breath. Stars were exploding behind her closed eyes. All she wanted to do was keep kissing these lips. She lost herself in all the sensations. She could smell the evergreens around them and the Christmas music weaved them in notes of joy. She could taste the cider on Vanessa's tongue; it was tart and sweet at the same time. As the stars continued to dart behind her closed eyelids she felt Vanessa's hands holding their bodies tightly, chest to chest. And then the best sensation of all was the love that beat from Vanessa's heart right into Makenna's. It was a *thump-thump* that crashed into her heart and filled it with love until it became staccato heartbeats like little wings carrying her love to Vanessa's. She never wanted this to end.

Vanessa finally pulled back so they both could grab a breath.

Her chest heaving, Makenna said, "Let's go home."

Vanessa nodded, thinking to herself that home was wherever she was with this incredible woman.

They walked quickly to the car, hand in hand, laughing and giggling the whole way. Makenna started the car and got the heater going. She looked over at Vanessa, her face serious but warm. "I love you. Now let's talk about this living arrangement you mentioned this morning."

The smile that overtook Vanessa's face couldn't have been any bigger. "Okay!"

"Let me say this. My house is just a house. It would become a home if you and Declan moved in."

"You'd want us both to move in with you?" Vanessa exclaimed, grabbing Makenna's free hand, the other on the steering wheel, guiding them home.

"Of course, if that's where you want us to live."

"That would be fine with me if that's where you want to live."

"What about your grandparents' place?"

"I asked you to help me with it because I hoped it could become ours. Does it feel like a home to you? Or do you have bad memories there?"

"I have wonderful memories there. It has always felt like a home. Your grandparents made it feel like that."

"Do you think if we redid it together we could make it ours? I realize it started as my grandparents', but I want it to be ours. I want you to feel like it's your home, too. *Ours.*"

"Hmm, do you think we could agree on what needs to be done?" Makenna asked hesitantly.

"Would you speak up and tell me what you think? Because if you won't then we do have one more option."

"What's that?"

"We can get a new place."

"We could, but if I did speak up, would you listen? Or just go along with whatever I said?"

Vanessa's eyes crinkled with amusement. "You know I'll listen, but you also know I won't just go along. When have I ever done that?"

Makenna laughed. "Just checking. I wanted to make sure you were being honest."

"I think we can redesign that house together and make it incredible, just like we are."

Makenna quickly looked over at her and smiled. "I do too." She kissed the back of Vanessa's hand just as her cell phone beeped.

Vanessa furrowed her brow. "That has to be Declan. Hope everything's okay," she said, digging her phone out of her purse.

"Well?"

Vanessa released a huge sigh.

"Babe, what's the matter? Is he okay?" Makenna asked warily.

"Unbelievable. It's like history repeating itself," she grumbled incredulously.

"What?"

"That's Declan. My mother is at the house."

"Holy shit! Are you kidding?"

"Nope."

Makenna turned onto the next street, heading for Vanessa's grandparents' house.

"Where are you going? That's not the way to your house."

"I know. We're going to yours."

It had been such a wonderful night and Vanessa didn't want her mother to ruin it. "We don't have to. I can deal with her tomorrow."

Makenna snorted. "No we can't." She pulled into Vanessa's driveway. "I need to tell you something before we go in," Makenna said, reaching for Vanessa's hand. She made sure Vanessa was looking at her before she continued. "Since we've found one another again, you keep saying you won't let anyone or anything come between us."

"I won't. Not again. I am not losing you," Vanessa said adamantly with tears in her eyes.

"You're not losing me. And you're not doing this alone. I will not let anyone come between us either, babe. We are in this together and we will handle your mother together."

"Really?"

"Yes. I'm sorry I haven't told you that earlier, but I have a say in this. And I'm not losing you again. We have a chance at an incredible life together and we're going to live it."

Vanessa released a breath and wiped the tears from her cheeks. "I love you, Makenna Markus." She took Makenna's face in her hands and quickly kissed her.

"I love you too," Makenna said with another quick kiss.

They got out of the car and walked up to the door, hand in hand as always.

13

W hen they walked into the house, Vanessa surveyed the scene before speaking. Her mother sat in the chair that Declan usually claimed while Declan stood in the doorway to the kitchen with an apologetic look on his face. Vanessa gave him a reassuring smile that turned to one of surprise when Makenna walked up next to her and spoke directly to her mother.

"Mrs. Perry, it's been a long time," she said with a relaxed smile.

"I should've known she was out with you," she spat.

"Mother, what are you doing here?" Vanessa asked, ignoring her comment.

"I could ask you the same thing, Vanessa."

"I'm here spending the holidays with my son. I told you I'm going to redo this house and I'm making plans for that." She smiled over at Declan then looked back at her mother with her eyebrows raised.

Mrs. Perry straightened up. "I came here because I wanted to be sure my grandson was all right and you weren't ruining his life."

Declan started to speak but Vanessa held up her hand. "Ruining his life," she said with a laugh. She decided she was going to make her mother say it. "And how am I ruining his life?"

Her mother sat up even straighter and looked down then back into Vanessa's eyes defiantly. "By running around with this woman."

"And how is that ruining Declan's life?"

Before Mrs. Perry could speak, Makenna took a step forward. She looked over at Declan and smiled. "Mrs. Perry, what are you afraid of?"

"Excuse me?" she said, taken aback.

"You seem to detest even the idea that Vanessa and I are friends. That type of reaction usually comes from fear. So I'll ask you again, what are you afraid of?"

"You two aren't *friends*. I know it's more than that."

"So why does that bother you, Gran?" Declan asked, his voice kind as he walked over to her. "I explained to you that Coach Markus has helped me more than anyone else to succeed this semester. She is a good person. I would think that you would want Mom to be with a good person."

"It's not that simple, Declan. You're too young to understand."

"No he's not, Mother. He understands that Makenna and I love each other and that there's nothing wrong with that."

"Nothing wrong with it!" she exclaimed. "What will people think?"

"I'll tell you what my friends think, Gran. They think my mom is lucky because Coach Markus is well respected here. And they think I'm lucky too."

"Your friends know?" Mrs. Perry said, shocked.

Vanessa looked at Makenna and shrugged. This was the first she'd heard about it.

After taking a deep breath, Vanessa began speaking slowly and clearly. "You did a terrible thing by keeping us apart twenty-five years ago. You used Makenna's reputation to manipulate me and force us apart. You should be ashamed, but I know you never will be. I told you fifteen years ago that you were done running my life. There is nothing you can say or do that will keep us apart any longer. If you plan to stay in my life then you need to find a way to accept Makenna because I love her and we're going to be together."

Mrs. Perry stared at the two of them, not saying anything.

Makenna's face softened. "Mrs. Perry, I know you were trying to do what you thought was best for your daughter. For twenty-five years we stayed apart and then finally five days ago we found one another again." She couldn't help but look at Vanessa, her smile radiating love. "We are meant to be. There's nothing and no one that will come between us from here on out."

Vanessa grabbed Makenna's hand, intertwining their fingers.

"You realize your father and sister won't have anything to do with you now," her mother threatened.

Vanessa snorted. "When have they ever had anything to do with me? Dad's only interested in my business success and Elizabeth is too busy with her club to have time to spend with me."

"But what about Declan and the girls?" she asked.

"The girls and Declan are busy with their own lives at their schools."

"Yeah Gran, I see Liza and Caroline at Thanksgiving. That's it."

Vanessa raised her eyebrow. "You don't seem to remember that you all pulled away from me after the divorce."

"That was your doing," her mother spat.

"I divorced Daniel—not my family, Mother," Vanessa fired back.

Makenna was beginning to realize that except for a few work friends, Vanessa had spent much of her time alone. It seems they both had ended up alone, their hearts meant only for the other.

Vanessa sighed. "This isn't going to change. You don't want to be in my life, that's obvious. Makenna and I are going to redo this house for us and Declan. I'm moving here and we're going to live happily ever after. I can't imagine why you wouldn't want that for your child because all I want for mine is for him to be happy. Makenna makes me happy. End of discussion." She didn't give her mother time to respond before she turned to Declan, continuing. "You are welcome to stay with us tonight over at Makenna's if you don't want to stay here with your grandmother."

Confident in her decisions, Vanessa turned back to her mother. "Mother, you can stay here tonight, but you need to go home tomorrow. I hope you have a merry Christmas with Dad and Elizabeth and her family. I will be here having the best Christmas I've ever had." She turned to Makenna and smiled as she squeezed her hand. Vanessa couldn't believe how calm she felt. Years of dread and sadness that had piled onto her shoulders had been lifted. Knowing Makenna was next to her, fighting for them with her, had made all the difference in the world.

Declan walked over and hugged his mom. "I'll stay here with Gran tonight. I'm going to make her understand that you and Makenna are good together and are good parents to me."

Vanessa hid her surprise at his words, but was so pleased. "You don't have to do that. I'm really over it. All I need is you and Makenna, and I've got that."

"I'll text you in the morning. I won't leave until I see you," Declan assured her.

Vanessa hugged him again. "Thanks for sticking up for me."

He smiled shyly, then went to Makenna and hugged her. "Merry Christmas, Coach."

Makenna couldn't have been more surprised. She hugged him back. "Merry Christmas, Declan."

They walked to the door and Makenna turned around before they left. "Merry Christmas, Mrs. Perry."

Vanessa looked at her mother and paused. She didn't know why she had let this woman keep her in fear all these years. But not anymore. "Goodbye, Mother."

They walked out the door hand in hand. Makenna was beginning to believe in Christmas miracles after all.

14

As they walked into Makenna's house she asked Vanessa, "Are you sure you're okay?"

Vanessa chuckled. "For the third time, yes babe. I'm okay."

"Sorry. I know that had to be hard."

"I actually expected it to be harder. I think deep down I knew she'd show up here. But," she swept Makenna into her arms as they walked into the living room, "It made a big difference knowing you were right beside me and you weren't afraid to speak up."

"Fear is what motivates so much of what we do. She's afraid of what people will think. She doesn't want to be looked down upon by her friends."

"When in actuality they probably couldn't care less," Vanessa pointed out. "All I know is that facing her with you and then Declan speaking up gave me strength. When we walked out of there I couldn't believe I let her scare me for so long. It was like I was seeing her for who she is. An old, scared, mean woman."

"But still, babe. That's your family."

Vanessa's face softened and she gently stroked Makenna's face with the back of her hand. "It does hurt, but my family won't accept me and I can't live the way they think I should." She looked deep into Makenna's eyes and found the family that had always been there. "All of that falls away as soon as I look into your eyes, hear your voice, or feel your touch. Sure, I wish everyone would accept us, but they won't. All I need is you, all I have to have is you. You, me and Declan are all the family I need."

She'd cupped Makenna's chin when she said those last words and now she held it firmly and claimed the only lips she'd ever wanted to kiss. The lips that fit perfectly with hers. The lips that stole her breath every time.

If Makenna had any doubts that Vanessa was upset they were gone as soon as their lips touched. Vanessa devoured her lips like they were a tasty delicacy on the finest menu. God, she loved this woman and wanted to show her in every way she could. She slowly pulled away and looked into Vanessa's dark brown eyes. Desire pooled into the depths of those chocolate orbs and it was all for her.

"If you'd do me a favor, we can get to the ending that we should have had twenty-five years ago."

"I'll do anything for you. Name it." Vanessa's voice was low and sultry. It seeped along Makenna's skin like syrup, thick and slow, and made her shiver with anticipation.

Makenna took a deep breath to gather herself. "There's wine in a decanter on the kitchen counter with two glasses. Would you pour us both a glass? I'll be right back."

Intrigued, Vanessa cocked her eyebrow, kissed Makenna gently on the cheek and sauntered into the kitchen, full well knowing Makenna was watching her hips sway.

Good God, Makenna couldn't pull her eyes away. When Vanessa was out of sight she shook her head and hurried to the bedroom.

Vanessa poured the wine, wondering what Makenna had planned. She didn't really care. All she wanted was to be in her arms.

Makenna came into the kitchen with a suggestive smile. She took her glass of wine in one hand and grabbed Vanessa's hand with the other. She led them down the hall and just inside her bedroom.

Vanessa gasped when she looked around the room. It was the

most romantic scene she'd ever laid her eyes on. There were poinsettias all around the room along with candles that gave off an evergreen scent mixed with cloves and allspice. A string of lights hung over the bed just like stars in the night sky. In the background music played faintly. It smelled, looked, and sounded like Christmas. She looked over at Makenna and could see the reflection of the candles in her eyes. The lights framed her from behind and she looked like an angel.

Wait, that wasn't Christmas music. She listened for a moment and tilted her head. "Is that..."

"Yep, our old playlist." Makenna grinned, pleased that Vanessa recognized it. "A toast," she said, holding up her glass. Vanessa held her glass up too.

"You've made me a believer in this Christmas miracle magic. It's incredible that we found one another again."

"And that you weren't angry at me with the way things were left," Vanessa added.

Makenna continued, "You didn't give up on us."

"And you gave us a chance," Vanessa said softly.

They clinked glasses and took a drink. Vanessa's eyes widened at the exquisite taste invading her mouth.

Makenna smiled, knowing she liked the wine. But they had all night to drink wine. She took Vanessa's glass and set it on the dresser along with hers.

She stood in front of Vanessa. A slow smile crept on her face. "If this was twenty-five years ago we'd both be naked already." She took her time looking from Vanessa's eyes to her mouth to how her hair fell beautifully down her shoulders in deep crimson waves. "But we've got all night." She began to slowly lean in and when their lips were a breath apart, she whispered, "I love you, Nessa."

Vanessa felt worshipped. Her lips longed for Makenna's. And when they finally touched hers, her body ignited. She couldn't breathe or think. All she could do was feel. Makenna's tongue languidly traced her lips, leaving wet fire behind, and when she finally slid her tongue inside her mouth Vanessa's moan was music to Makenna's ears. She felt Makenna's hands on her sweater and she began to pull it up. Their lips parted briefly so she could pull it up over her head. Vanessa did the same with Makenna's sweater, their lips still pressed together.

"I could kiss you forever," Makenna whispered.

"You'd better," Vanessa responded, her hands at the front of Makenna's pants. She felt Makenna stop her and pulled back to look in her eyes.

Makenna's gaze pierced through Vanessa to her core. She felt a tug in her center and had never wanted her more. Makenna made quick work of both their pants and stepped back to admire this beautiful woman. The scarlet colored bra with black lace offered Vanessa's breasts up to Makenna like a cherished treasure. The matching low cut bikini undies made Makenna's heart pound that much harder.

"You are so beautiful," she purred. Makenna took her finger and traced it from Vanessa's shoulder, across her collarbone and down into her cleavage. Her skin was hot to the touch and goosebumps appeared as her finger continued down Vanessa's stomach and hooked lazily into her waistband. Makenna's eyes retraced the path of her finger and rested on Vanessa's chest as it rose and fell with anticipation.

Makenna pulled Vanessa to her with the finger tugging at her panties, stretching them. "My heart is full of love for you, Nessa. Let me pour it out over you."

Vanessa could feel her insides tighten and knees weaken at Makenna's words. She almost came right then.

Makenna leaned in and kissed Vanessa's neck before lazily kissing down to her collarbone. She licked her breasts with the tip of her tongue, outlining the top of her bra. Vanessa dropped her head back and released a breath. "Good God, Kenna," she whispered.

She backed toward the bed pulling Vanessa with her, using that single finger in her undies. The finger came out and Vanessa immediately missed it. But Makenna lowered both Vanessa's bra straps and worshipped her with her eyes. She reached around and unclasped her bra, freeing her full breasts. Makenna placed her hand at either side of Vanessa's breasts and rubbed her thumbs over her hardened nipples.

Again Vanessa threw her head back, basking in Makenna's touch, wanting it all. She felt Makenna swing her around so the back of her legs touched the foot of the bed. She gently pushed her down onto the bed and while she glided up to the pillows, Makenna quickly removed her bra and undies. Vanessa watched as Makenna's eyes washed over her. She slowly climbed up the bed, Vanessa spreading her legs so Makenna could settle between them. She lowered her breasts and Vanessa could feel her nipples graze her belly just above her hairline. Then Makenna slid up Vanessa's body until they were chest to chest.

Vanessa had to touch her. She ran her hands down Makenna's back, trying to draw her closer. She spread her legs wider and slid her hands down to Makenna's butt and pulled her center towards hers. The instant wet heat hit her she groaned.

"I adore you," Makenna softly crooned.

"I need you," Vanessa pleaded. She didn't think she'd ever wanted Makenna more.

"I'm here. I'll always be here."

This brought tears to Vanessa's eyes, but they were quickly forgotten as Makenna crashed her lips onto Vanessa's. This kiss was full of passion, but also promise, and eternal commitment. Vanessa buried her hands in Makenna's hair as their kiss broke and Makenna's lips travelled everywhere.

Makenna kissed her neck, her chest; she swirled around her nipples and then bit down. Vanessa was on fire. Her knees were bent and splayed open, wanting Makenna lower. She continued kissing her way down Vanessa's body and paused to inhale her scent, musky and aromatic. The tip of her tongue touched just above her opening and slid up and down through her folds tasting the sharp, tangy sweetness that was her Vanessa.

Her moans grew louder with every swipe of Makenna's tongue.

"Oh yes, baby. Fucking yes," she murmured. Makenna smiled briefly because Vanessa always swore when they were making love, but rarely did otherwise. She circled around Vanessa's opening and then found her pulsating clit waiting for her to suck it into her mouth.

Vanessa thought she was in heaven when Makenna took her into her mouth. But when she slid two fingers inside Vanessa was in ecstasy. "Oh fuck," she moaned loudly.

Makenna began a rhythm, moving in and out slowly while she continued to suck Vanessa into her mouth. She began to speed up her fingers as Vanessa's hips matched the rhythm.

Vanessa reached down and pulled Makenna's head up to her lips. She was close, but she wanted her arms around Makenna and wanted her own tongue in Makenna's mouth now. She held them chest to chest and bathed Makenna's mouth in love with her tongue. She could feel Makenna's love wherever their bodies touched, rushing inside her, filling her up to overflowing.

Makenna felt Vanessa tighten and pushed in deeper. Vanessa buried her face in Makenna's hair and clutched her even closer. She hummed, "I love you, I love you, I love you," over and over.

Vanessa felt the orgasm spread over her entire body. Her arms and legs were warmed from the inside out. Her core exploded in warm wetness as her heart opened and took in all the love Makenna could give her. She held on, not wanting it to end. When she couldn't hold on any longer she fell back on the bed, her arms out wide, beads of sweat on her brow and a brilliant smile on her face.

She felt before she heard Makenna chuckle. Opening one eye, she saw Makenna gently run her thumb over her brow, wiping the sweat. She opened the other eye and was amazed at the glow on Makenna's face. "You really do adore me," she said.

Makenna looked down into her eyes, "I really do."

Vanessa wrapped her arms around her. "I love you so, Kenna." The tears stung the back of her eyes again. She ran a hand through Makenna's brown hair as she looked up into the most beautiful face smiling down on her.

They both knew this was a significant moment, righting the

wrongs from the past. "I've always known you love me and I've always felt it, but it's truly never ending," Vanessa continued reverently.

"Christmas miracle?" Makenna said softly.

"Nope. We were meant to be."

15

The next morning they drove into Vanessa's driveway and her mother's car was gone.

"It's probably a good thing she's gone," Vanessa said, giggling.

Makenna looked over at her amused, but also wondering. "Why's that?"

"Because the way we're glowing she'd know what we were up to all night."

It was Makenna's turn to giggle. "It was an incredible night."

Vanessa leaned over and kissed Makenna slow and soft. "Mmm and there's many more nights like that to come."

Makenna sighed. "I'm ready."

They smiled at one another and got out of the car. Hand in hand they walked up to the front door. "Declan may not be up yet," Vanessa said, quiet as they entered the house. She was surprised to immediately smell coffee.

"Good morning," Vanessa called.

"In here," Declan yelled from the kitchen. They walked in and found Declan cooking waffles.

Vanessa was surprised. "What are you doing?"

"What's it look like? I'm cooking waffles. I figured you two would be here sometime this morning and I wanted to cook you breakfast." He filled a cup of coffee and handed it to Makenna. "Here, Makenna."

"Thanks Declan," she said, both eyebrows climbing up her forehead.

"Here, Mom," he said, handing Vanessa coffee in a mug that said *World's Greatest Mom.*

Vanessa took a small sip of the hot liquid. "How was your night?"

"Well, I recognized what Coach did last night with Gran, asking about her fear. I remember discussing it in our sessions."

Vanessa and Makenna exchanged a glance. "And?" Vanessa prodded gently.

"I don't think she is necessarily against gay people. I think she doesn't want it in her family because she is so stuck on how she is viewed. I tried to explain to her that I really didn't think her friends or her precious club would give a shit, but I didn't get through."

"I hope she didn't give you a hard time because you don't have a problem with us."

"I do have a problem with it though."

Vanessa's stomach dropped. "What do you mean?" Makenna walked over next to her and put an arm around her waist protectively.

"It makes me so mad that she kept you apart. Now granted, I probably wouldn't be here if she hadn't, but it's wrong to do that to another person, especially your own kid."

Vanessa was surprised at how upset he was.

"Look, Declan," Makenna said, walking over to him. "This is a bit like what we've talked about on meet days."

He looked at her, thinking back to their sessions. "You control the things you can on meet days and don't worry about the things you can't."

"Exactly. The only way your grandmother is going to change her mind is if *she* does it. I appreciate you trying because I know how much you love your mom, but don't worry about us." She looked over at Vanessa then back to Declan. "I promise you we're living our happily-ever-after now and we'll take care of one another."

"Other people may not understand or approve of our relation-ship," Vanessa added. "All that matters to us is that you do. That you know we're a family, the three of us. You, me and Makenna."

"I do," he said, nodding. A mischievous smile spread across his face and he looked to Makenna. "I promise I won't call you Mom on campus, Coach."

Makenna's eyes almost popped out of her head.

Laughter erupted from Vanessa and Declan joined in. "It's okay, Coach. I was kidding," he said, coming over and patting her on the back while Vanessa was doubled over laughing.

"Oh, I see how you two are. This is how it's going to be, huh. Well, you both need me, so you might want to rethink ganging up on me."

"Sorry, Coach," Declan said, trying to stop laughing. "I couldn't resist. And your face! You should have seen it."

Makenna smirked at him.

"I couldn't pick a better bonus mom, Makenna. Seriously, welcome to the family. I know you'll make my mom very happy and she deserves it."

Makenna couldn't help but smile at him. "Thank you Declan. I guess you'll be an okay son," she deadpanned.

This time his eyes widened and he laughed. "I deserved that. Well played." He hesitated before adding, "Mom."

"And you—" Makenna started, turning to Vanessa.

Vanessa quickly kissed her before she could say anything else. Declan whistled and whooped.

Makenna pulled back and leered at Vanessa. "Not fair."

"Sorry not sorry. We have a lot of kisses to catch up on."

"Come on, Moms," Declan interrupted. "The waffles are ready. Let's eat."

They sat down at the table, still chuckling while filling their plates.

"Hey, these are good," Makenna said between bites.

"Thanks. I learned a little from Mom in the kitchen."

Vanessa smiled, obviously proud.

"What do you have going today? Don't you meet the parents tomorrow?" Declan asked.

"Yes and I'm nervous," Vanessa said honestly.

"What? Why are you nervous? You practically lived at my house. They already know you," Makenna reminded her.

"Don't be nervous, Mom. Mr. Markus is really a cool old guy."

"You know him?" Vanessa said, shocked.

"He came to practice a couple of times. He's nice."

"He used to pole vault back when he was in school and loves to come watch practice," Makenna explained. "What was it he told you, Declan?"

"He said that if he'd had the technology and equipment that I have today that he'd be able to jump eighteen feet too." Declan imitated an older man's voice.

Makenna laughed. "He loves to see how technology has improved the sport."

"He could probably have done it too. He looks like he's still in pretty good shape. Don't worry Mom, he'll love you," Declan said, turning to Vanessa. "And if it gets awkward just tell him that I'm your son. He'll remember me."

Vanessa looked at him, dumbstruck.

Makenna chuckled. "He's right, my dad will remember him. He asks me about you."

"See," he said, chewing and looking at his mom innocently.

"But that's not until tomorrow. Why would you think they wouldn't like you?" Makenna asked.

"Oh, I don't know," Vanessa said nonchalantly. "Maybe because I broke their daughter's heart!" she exclaimed.

Makenna smiled compassionately. "But you're also the one that put it back together. And you're the one that's made me so happy!"

Vanessa looked at her, still unsure.

"Aww, this is so sweet. Is this how it is when you're in love?" Declan teased.

"Don't play, mister. You'll see how it feels someday and we'll be right there to make fun of you!" Vanessa chided.

"We sure will," Makenna agreed.

Declan laughed and held up his hands at them in surrender. "Okay, okay. I'll probably need your help when that happens."

"Hmm, we might help out. I guess," Makenna said, winking at Vanessa.

"So if that's tomorrow, what are you doing today?"

"Do we have to do anything?" Makenna asked.

"What do you mean?" Vanessa asked.

"I think it'd be nice to sit around the house. Watch a movie, talk. I am on holiday after all."

"I know something we could do at home," Vanessa said suggestively.

"Oh please, wait until I leave," Declan said, pretending to throw up.

"Oh my God, I don't mean that, Declan," Vanessa corrected him.

"What did you mean?"

"Yeah, what did you mean?" Makenna asked.

"Well, I noticed you don't have a Christmas tree at your place. I think it would be fun to decorate one. It is our first Christmas together."

"You should be able to get a good deal on one today," Declan said, amused.

"You know, that might be fun. I think I could find my decorations. I haven't put one up in years," Makenna said.

"We have some old ones here that were my grandparents'. I'm sure between the two of us we could create a festive tree. What do you think?"

"I think that reminds me—I left something in my purse," Makenna said, hopping up and going into the living room.

She came back in with a small package wrapped in holiday paper. "Merry Christmas, Declan," she said, handing the package to him.

"Makenna!" he said surprised. "I was just kidding about a Christmas present."

Makenna chuckled. "I know that. I saw this and thought of you. Open it."

Declan unwrapped the snow globe. A huge smile spread across his face and he shook it mightily. "I love it! That looks just like me!"

"That's what I thought. It's one of your trail runs through the snow."

"I'll put it on my desk in the dorm." He got up and came over to her. "Thank you." He wrapped her in a hug.

"Your welcome."

He kept shaking it with a smile on his face. Vanessa caught Makenna's eye and winked at her.

Makenna got up and started to clear the table. "You cooked, I'll clean up."

"I'll finish packing so I can get on the road," Declan said. "Thanks again, Makenna."

After he walked out, Vanessa stood and pulled Makenna into a hug.

"Did you feel it?" she asked.

"Feel it?" Makenna repeated.

"This felt just like family to me," Vanessa said, obviously pleased.

Makenna's face lit up. "It did, didn't it."

Vanessa kissed her gently. "I'd say you nailed it, bonus mom."

"Bonus mom," Makenna snorted.

They both laughed and began to clean up the kitchen.

16

D eclan was right. They got a Christmas tree for free at the lot near the university. They strapped it to the top of Makenna's car and made it home without losing it.

Earlier they had loaded a couple of boxes of Christmas decorations from Vanessa's grandparents into Makenna's car and gone by her house to see what she had. In the garage she found a box labeled "decorations" and thought maybe there would be a few Christmas ones in it.

"I know I have lights somewhere," Makenna said as they unloaded the tree. "We can always use the ones in my room if we have to."

"I don't know, those were awfully festive and sexy last night and come to think of it, this morning too," she said, winking at Makenna from the other end of the tree.

Makenna smiled and stopped walking. "Last night was incredible."

"It sure was. Let's get this Christmas tree up and make some more magic."

"You sure believe in this Christmas magic," Makenna said as they walked up to her porch.

"I thought you were a believer now, too."

"You know what I believe in," she said, opening the door and watching her cats run out. "I believe in us."

"I do too, but a little magic couldn't hurt."

Makenna chuckled as they wrestled the tree into the house. They brought the boxes in and went to work placing the tree in its stand and looking through the decorations. Makenna found the lights and they strung them around the tree.

"Okay babe, hold up," Vanessa said, looking around. "Where's the ornament we bought last night?"

"It's right here," Makenna said, walking in from the kitchen, dangling it from her fingers.

Vanessa's eyes lit up. "That has to be the first one we put on the tree every year."

"Let's do it together." She reached out but then brought the ornament back. "I'm so glad Declan's not here. I can just hear him."

Vanessa laughed. "Don't let him bother you. But he is having way too much fun with this."

Makenna laughed too. "I don't care. I love every sappy minute I get to spend with you."

"Me too," Vanessa said softly.

Vanessa put her hand over Makenna's as she hung the ornament on the tree. They stepped back and Vanessa put her arms around Makenna from behind, resting her head on her shoulder. Makenna leaned back and put her hands over Vanessa's. They gazed at the ornament, feeling all the promise and love the future held.

"Let's get this finished so we can sit on the couch and admire our work. I'll make us hot chocolate."

Makenna turned in her arms. "Not so fast, Mrs. Claus." She leaned in and pressed her lips softly to Vanessa's. The kiss heated up when their tongues met and they pulled one another closer. After a few moments Makenna pulled back, letting out a deep breath. "We're a fucking Hallmark Christmas card. Look at us, kissing in front of the tree after hanging our first ornament together."

"I love it," Vanessa said, swatting Makenna on the ass. "Let's get this done."

"Yes ma'am, Mrs. Claus," Makenna said, saluting.

They looked through the boxes at the different decorations and chose together which ones made the tree. There were several in Vanessa's grandparents' box that she remembered and Makenna told her the history behind several of her own.

When they were finished Vanessa started to make hot chocolate from scratch while Makenna started a fire. She grabbed a blanket and tossed it on the couch. The cats came running in, ready for their food, when she opened the door. Together they got the cats fed and hot chocolate made, then settled on the couch.

"I have to say this is one beautiful room. My house has never looked or smelled this good."

"It's so cozy. The tree twinkling, fire crackling; hot chocolate and snuggling with my baby. What a perfect night."

They leaned back shoulder to shoulder and sat in a comfortable silence.

"Tomorrow we go to your folks in the evening, right?"

"Yep."

"When does your family open presents?"

"Christmas morning."

"So, I can't give you your present tomorrow night."

"Nope, it won't be Christmas."

Vanessa chuckled. "For someone who doesn't like Christmas, you kind of have your rules."

"When do you want me to give you your gift?"

Vanessa inhaled. "You got me a present?"

"Yes." Makenna grinned. "You know I did."

"I had one for you all those years ago."

"You did? Wow, I haven't thought about that. We were going to exchange gifts that night."

"We were," Vanessa said wistfully.

"What'd you get me?" Makenna asked, a childlike intrigue in her voice.

"I got you a necklace."

"You did? Aww, babe."

"Yeah, my mother found that too so I don't know what happened to it. What did you get me?" Vanessa asked, a little sad.

"Wait, do you remember what the necklace looked like?"

"I sure do. It was a single pearl surrounded by a little gold heart. It was to signify our pure love."

"Oh my God, Nessa. That's beautiful." She set their mugs on the table and took Vanessa's face in her hands. "Thank you." She kissed her tenderly with such compassion and love.

Vanessa smiled when Makenna pulled away. "You didn't even get it."

"I don't care, that's the sweetest thing anyone has ever done for me."

"I'm sure it's not. But you're welcome," she said, chuckling. "Now, what did you get me?"

Makenna gazed into Vanessa's eyes, contemplating her next move. She tilted her head and kept looking. Vanessa raised one eyebrow. "I'll be right back." She jumped up and went to her bedroom. After a few moments she came back with something in her closed hand.

"This should have been my first clue that I wasn't ever going to get over you," she said, sitting down to face Vanessa. "Do you remember how much you liked blue?"

"Of course I do, still do."

"Well, I got you a blue sapphire ring that was crazy expensive at the time for a kid in high school." She giggled. "But it would be considered cheap for us adults now."

"It doesn't matter how much it cost. You knew I loved blue, babe. That's sweet."

"Actually, I still have it."

Vanessa's eyes lit up as she inhaled loudly. "You do! Let me see, let me see."

Makenna opened her hand and in her palm was the sapphire ring. Vanessa ogled it and then looked at Makenna.

"Put it on me!" she said excitedly.

Makenna did as she was asked and slipped the ring on Vanessa's ring finger of her left hand.

"Look at that! It fits," Vanessa said, looking at it closely then holding her hand away and showing it off.

"You don't have to wear it. I mean look at it!" Makenna protested.

"I most certainly am going to wear it. I love it!" She turned to Makenna and wrapped her arms around her neck. "Thank you."

"You're welcome."

Vanessa's face turned serious. "I love you, Ken. I always have. And I'm going to show you every day from now on."

"You already do, Nessa."

She gave her a firm kiss then asked, "What about Christmas Day? Are we spending all day with your folks?"

"No. We'll hang out tomorrow evening for Christmas Eve dinner. Then we'll go back the next morning and open gifts with Christmas lunch to follow. Usually after that everyone passes out for a nap."

"Would you want to do a hike that afternoon?"

"I'd love to. We'll need it after everything my mom feeds us."

"Okay. I want you to take me back to those trees. They've been calling to me."

"Oh they have? Are the trees magical now too?"

"Those are and you know it."

Makenna stilled. "I do. They are."

Vanessa smiled. "Now, how about we get take-out and have a picnic?"

"I like that idea. Where do you want to have a picnic?"

"In bed."

Makenna raised her eyebrows. "I *love* that idea. Let me get the menus." She kissed Vanessa quickly, jumped up and hurried to the kitchen.

Vanessa watched her, marveling that this woman still loved her. The conversation she'd had with Declan yesterday afternoon, before Makenna had picked her up, was in the front of her mind. That afternoon hike had the potential to make this the best Christmas ever. She could hardly wait.

17

Vanessa pulled into Makenna's parents' driveway, her heart beating fast and butterflies in her stomach. Makenna looked over at her and took her hand.

"Babe, you don't have to be nervous."

"That's easy for you to say. My mother is a monster and it doesn't matter if she likes you; she doesn't even like me. I *want* your mom to like me!"

Makenna chuckled. "Come here," she said, pulling Vanessa to her.

"Should we be doing this in your parent's driveway?"

Makenna answered her with a kiss. It was gentle but firm and calmed Vanessa's anxiety.

She pulled back and smiled. "Thanks. I needed that."

"Anytime," Makenna said, winking.

They walked up hand in hand and Makenna called out when she opened the door. "Hey Mom, hi Dad."

"Come on in!" Doug Markus walked into the living room. "Hi sweetie," he said, hugging Makenna. He smiled at Vanessa over Makenna's shoulder.

"Dad, this is—" Makenna started, but her dad interrupted.

"Vanessa. It's so nice to see you again," he said with a broad smile on his face.

"Hi Mr. Markus, it's nice to see you."

Makenna's mother walked in, wiping her hands on a cup towel. "Hi hon," she said to Makenna and looked over at Vanessa. "Hello, Vanessa." Her smile didn't quite reach her eyes.

"Hi Mrs. Markus, thanks for including me tonight."

Jean Markus nodded. "Have a seat."

Makenna looked at her mother warily, not sure what to think. She had talked to her about Vanessa and she knew they were giving this another chance. Makenna thought her mom would be happy about it, but her behavior indicated otherwise.

Vanessa didn't seem to notice as Doug had shown her to the couch and he sat in his chair. They were talking about Vanessa's job and Makenna sat down next to her, watching her mom. Thank goodness her dad was a natural conversationalist. He loved to ask questions and could talk about almost anything.

Makenna heard Vanessa tell her dad, "I hear you've met my son, Declan."

"I have. He is a talented athlete."

"He didn't get it from me, I'm sure." Vanessa laughed.

Makenna's mom said, "I made eggnog. Would you like some?"

"She makes the best eggnog," Doug told Vanessa.

"I'd love some," Vanessa replied.

"Here, Mom. Let me help you," Makenna said, making eye contact with Vanessa, knowing she would be fine with her dad. Vanessa smiled, letting her know she was okay.

She walked into the kitchen with her mom and watched her pour the liquid into glasses. Makenna reached for the nutmeg and said, "What's wrong, Mom? You're not acting very happy to see us."

Jean bristled and turned toward Makenna, "I don't want you to get hurt again. I remember what happened all those years ago, Makenna. You're my daughter and there's nothing worse than when your child is in pain and you can't do anything about it."

"Mom, I appreciate that, but this time is different. It's up to us to make this work and we're both committed."

"I'm not going to let anyone or anything come between us ever again, Mrs. Markus," Vanessa said from the doorway.

Makenna and her mom both turned around as Vanessa walked in.

"My mother did a terrible thing to us and I was weak and afraid. But by some Christmas miracle we have been given another chance," she said, walking over to Makenna. She put her arm around her waist. "I understand your apprehension and I agree that there's nothing worse than when your child is in pain. But all I want for Makenna is happiness and that's what I intend to give her."

"Will you give us a chance?" Makenna asked her mom.

Jean studied them and her eyes rested on Vanessa's. She didn't look away, and Jean saw determination and fire in those eyes, but she also saw love. There was love for her daughter and Jean knew that was what Makenna wanted most.

"It doesn't matter now, but I wish I'd known back then." She paused. "I only want both of you to be happy; that's what mothers want. You know that, Vanessa," she said, looking directly at her.

"Vanessa makes me happy, Mom."

Jean's face softened. "I know that, sweetie." Jean sighed and looked at Vanessa, a tentative smile on her face. "Welcome back."

Makenna and Vanessa looked at one another, their faces hopeful.

Jean smiled at them both. "Now, let's have eggnog."

"What's taking so long in here?" Doug asked, standing in the doorway.

"Just a little girl-talk," Jean said, winking and handing him a glass of eggnog.

"Let's have a toast." He took the glass and smiled at his wife.

Makenna and Vanessa raised their glasses, waiting.

"This one," Doug gestured toward Makenna, "Never did believe in Santa's magic, but I think she may have finally changed her mind. Here's to Christmas miracles."

They clinked their glasses and took hearty drinks. Makenna

grinned at her dad. "You're right. But I'm a believer now because I think I'm living right in the middle of one."

They all laughed.

"Come on, let's go in here and make plans for tomorrow," Jean said, leading the way into the living room.

After another glass of eggnog they sat down for dinner. The conversation turned to Vanessa and her job, as Jean loved to cook. They also talked about how many athletes Makenna had helped and how the university's results had improved when they assigned each sport its own counselor.

Vanessa had no idea what all Makenna did for her students and athletes. She knew she helped Declan but Doug explained how she had helped other athletes get over fears that affected their performance. Makenna downplayed her role, but Vanessa glowed with pride as she listened to stories from Doug.

When they'd finished, Makenna and Vanessa hopped up to do the dishes.

"Jean, I hope you'll share this recipe for your mac and cheese. It was so decadent."

"Hmm, does that mean it could show up in one of your meal kits?"

"I don't know," Vanessa said thoughtfully. "Do you want it to?"

"I'm not sure."

"I really want to make it for Declan, but we could just come here once a week and you make it for us," Vanessa suggested.

Jean chuckled. "We might make that happen. Or you could get Makenna to make it. Don't let her fool you, Vanessa, she's quite the cook herself."

"Thank you for that information," she said, bumping hips with Makenna as they loaded the dishwasher.

Once everything was cleaned up, they all sat down in the living room together.

"What time will Luke and his crew be here tomorrow?"

"Those boys may be getting older, but they'll be up early to open presents," Jean said. "I'm planning to have lunch at one."

"Do we need to come early to help with anything?" asked Vanessa.

"Thank you, Vanessa, but I have everything ready to go."

"Are you sure we couldn't bring something? I can make a pie in the morning."

"Do we have the ingredients to make a pie? I'm not sure the stores will still be open," Makenna pointed out.

"I have everything for a pecan pie at the house," Vanessa answered.

"Oh Mom, you might want to take her up on that. She made one for Declan and it was out of this world."

"I don't want you to have to make a pecan pie in the morning."

"It's no trouble, really. It would make me feel better if you'd let me bring something."

"I say yes," Doug said. "I happen to love pecan pie."

Jean smiled at him. "I know you do. But you also love Italian cream cake and that's what I made this afternoon."

"My pants are getting tighter the longer I listen to you all talk," Makenna said, groaning.

"You can go run after lunch. You'll be fine," Jean stated.

"We are planning on going on a hike after lunch."

"I'm not surprised." Jean winked at Vanessa.

"Don't be that way, Mom, or I'll drag you with us."

"No way. Tomorrow is for indulgence."

Vanessa chuckled. She really liked Makenna's parents. After her declaration to Jean, they had made her feel welcome and part of the family; just like they had twenty-five years ago.

"Well, if we're making a pie in the morning we'd better get going and be sure you have everything," Makenna said to Vanessa.

"We? Are you going to help?" asked Vanessa, surprised.

"I sure will. I take directions well."

"Okay then." They got up and started toward the door.

"Thank you for having me tonight. I really enjoyed it," Vanessa said to Makenna's parents.

"We're glad you could be with us and tomorrow, too." Doug got up and walked them to the door, Jean at his side.

"See you in the morning," Makenna said, hugging them both.

"See you tomorrow, Vanessa. Merry Christmas," Jean said, pulling her into a hug.

Tears stung Vanessa's eyes. She couldn't remember the last time her mother had hugged her.

"Thank you. Merry Christmas to you both," Vanessa said as Makenna took her hand and led them to the car.

Once inside Makenna turned to her. "Are you all right?"

"I'm more than all right, babe. I love your parents."

Makenna chuckled, "Yeah, I hit the jackpot with those two. And I can tell they love you, too."

"One more Christmas miracle?"

Makenna groaned. "Yessss, one more Christmas miracle."

Vanessa backed out of the driveway, not remembering a time when she'd looked forward to Christmas this much. She felt like a little kid waiting for Santa, only she would be Santa tomorrow, hopefully making all their dreams come true.

18

Vanessa could feel Makenna pressed to her back, her arm lazily wrapped around her stomach. She could happily wake up like this the rest of her life. A smile crept across her face as she thought about the day to come. They'd exchange gifts this morning, she'd make the pie, they'd go eat at Makenna's parents' and she'd meet the rest of the family. Then after lunch they were hiking to the love trees.

At least that's what she called them. Over the years those trees had grown and wrapped themselves around one another. Each supported the other and without each other, they would fall. It reminded her of their love. Even apart their love had grown and maybe it was wrapped around each of them so strongly that it had finally pulled them together. She had big plans at those trees today.

They had a lot to do before they got there though. She smiled and gently rolled onto her back then over on her other side. She looked into Makenna's beautiful face, so peaceful in sleep. This brought her back twenty-five years; she could still see the young woman and just as she had then, she hoped Makenna was dreaming of them now.

"Mmm, I can feel you looking at me," Makenna said sleepily, her eyes fluttering open.

"Good morning gorgeous. Merry Christmas."

Makenna smiled. "Merry Christmas." She reached her lips to Vanessa's and pecked her sweetly.

"Were you dreaming of us?"

"As a matter of fact I was."

"Ooww, tell me."

"I dreamed it was Christmas morning and you wouldn't let me out of this bed to open my presents."

"Your dream is coming true because I'm not letting you out of this bed," Vanessa said, rolling on top of her.

"What about our presents and the pie and my family?" she said, rubbing her hands up and down Vanessa's back.

"We won't be late. I have a little Christmas gift to give you first," Vanessa said with a wicked smile. She captured Makenna's lips and woke her up with a scorching kiss. When she pulled away. "I love you, Kenna," she said breathlessly.

"I love you too," she said, pulling Vanessa back down for another passionate kiss.

They were interrupted when Vanessa's ringtone blasted through the room.

"That's Declan. Wow, it's early for him," she said, reaching for the phone. "Oh no, he's FaceTiming us!"

They both sat up instantly. Makenna leaned over the side of the bed and grabbed her shirt, throwing it at Vanessa. "Here," she giggled.

Vanessa quickly put it on and connected the call while Makenna jumped up to find another shirt.

"Merry Christmas!" Vanessa said, chuckling.

"Merry Christmas, Mom! Are you still in bed?" he said cheerily.

Makenna leaned in next to her so she could see him. "Santa doesn't make us get up early around here."

Declan laughed. "I didn't think he did here either, but some girls around here couldn't wait. How did things go last night? They love you, don't they, Mom?"

Vanessa looked over at Makenna and grinned. "It was touch and go for a minute, but then I told them I was Declan Sommerfield's mom and they immediately loved me."

Declan laughed. "Hey, have you opened your gifts yet?"

"Not yet," they both said, eyeing one another.

"Hey, do you know what we both got?" asked Makenna, just realizing this.

"Heck yeah. That's why I wanted to know."

"They are still under the tree."

"Well, I'll let you go open them. Call me back when you do. Okay?"

"You sure are interested in this," Vanessa said suspiciously.

"It's because I know you're both going to love it."

Vanessa and Makenna both looked at him skeptically.

"Go! Call me back. Bye, love you both." He disconnected the call.

Vanessa was laughing. "He knows how to liven up a room!" She looked over at Makenna who was sitting there with a dazed, slight smile on her face. "Babe? Are you all right?" she asked, immediately concerned. She angled in front of Makenna. "Kenna! What is it?"

She finally looked into Vanessa's eyes. "Did you hear him? He said 'love you both.'" Makenna had tears in her eyes. "I had no idea how utterly incredible it would make me feel to hear him say that."

Vanessa tilted her head and gathered Makenna in her arms. "Oh baby, he loved you before I came back to town. I could tell the way he talked about you. But now, he loves you because you're his new momma!"

Makenna laughed through her tears. "That isn't even funny."

"Then why are you laughing?" Vanessa leaned back so she could look into Makenna's eyes. "I never wanted him to call another woman Mom. But with you, it's natural. I know he feels it. I do too. And it fills my heart to overflowing."

Makenna smiled and shook her head. "Please don't say it."

"Say what?" Vanessa's brow furrowed.

"Another Christmas miracle."

Vanessa fell back on the bed, laughing. Makenna jumped up and hovered over her.

"I want to open my present! Please!"

Vanessa giggled. "Well, I can't get up, someone's got me pinned down."

Makenna smirked, leaned down and kissed her hard. Their lips smacked and Makenna jumped up off the bed. She turned around and looked at her. "Well, are you coming?"

Vanessa took off and over her shoulder yelled, "Race you!"

"Hold it!" Makenna shouted.

Vanessa grabbed the doorknob and stopped. "What?"

Makenna looked pointedly at Vanessa's lower body. Vanessa looked down and realized all she had on was a T-shirt. Makenna held up her sleep shorts. "You might need these."

"Thanks," she said after Makenna tossed them to her.

They walked into the living room hand in hand, still laughing.

"I can already tell this is going to be the best Christmas ever," Makenna said, fetching their gifts from under the tree.

They sat on the couch, side by side. "You go first," Makenna said.

"No you go first. I already have the ring you gave me twenty five-years ago, so it's your turn."

Makenna furrowed her brow and shook her head. "I'm not sure I follow your logic, but okay." She unwrapped the box to find another box inside. Her eyebrows shot up her forehead.

"You know it's Declan's idea."

She giggled. "Of course it is." She began to open the smaller box and when she took the top off the box she gasped. "Oh my God, Nessa. It's beautiful!" Makenna stared down at a silver infinity necklace. Inside the loops were two tiny gems. She recognized one as Vanessa's birthstone, but wasn't sure about the other.

"You probably remember that this is my birthstone."

Makenna nodded, dreamily admiring the necklace.

"The other is Declan's."

Makenna's eyes, full of questions, shot up to meet Vanessa's.

"It was his idea. He said we're a family now and hoped you'd like it."

Makenna had tears in her eyes. She thought her heart might burst—it was so full of love, joy, and happiness.

"Here, let me put it on you."

"I've never seen anything like it, babe. It's beautiful. You know I'll never take it off."

Vanessa chuckled. "I know," she said softly, clasping it behind her neck.

Makenna leaned over and tenderly kissed Vanessa. "Oh, how I love you." She gazed intently into her eyes. "Thank you."

"You're welcome," Vanessa whispered and kissed her back just as tenderly.

Makenna sighed then remembered Vanessa's gift. She laughed softly. "Here, open yours."

Vanessa looked at her suspiciously. "Is it funny?"

"Not at all. You'll see. Open it, babe."

Vanessa eyed her but tore into the package like a kid at Christmas. She opened the small box and gasped just like Makenna had. "It's—" she paused as she took the ring out of the box. "It's exquisite," she said, peering at the silver band that looped together to create the infinity sign. Inside each loop was a diamond. Vanessa chuckled. "Now I see why you laughed. Looks like great minds think alike."

"Or we both know this is forever."

Vanessa looked up. "This is forever."

Makenna smiled. "Look inside the band."

Vanessa squinted and read the inscription. "It's a date." She thought about it for a moment then looked at Makenna, confused. "Why would you choose the day my mother ruined us? Wait..." she said, remembering the stroll, and then it came to her. "That's the night I told you that you were my girl. That's the night I told you I'd always love you."

"That's right. That was the night we promised one another."

"We did," Vanessa said, nodding and remembering those words that night. She could still feel the love she had for Makenna that night. And now it was even stronger. "Would you?" she asked Makenna, handing her the ring to put on her finger.

"Will you give me that cheap little blue sapphire back?"

"No I will not!" Vanessa said, pulling her hand back.

"Come on, babe," Makenna grabbed at her hand and took the sapphire ring off. She sighed and then put it on her right hand. She took the infinity ring and slipped it on her left ring finger. The symbolism was not lost on either one of them.

Vanessa held her hand out, gazing at the ring. To her the diamonds shone bright like the love in their hearts for one another. "Thank you, Ken." She leaned in and put her lips a breath away from Makenna's. "Merry Christmas," she whispered, their eyes locked.

"Merry Christmas," Makenna whispered back.

Vanessa brought their lips together. Soft, firm, the only lips she ever wanted to kiss. She pulled away slightly. "Let's go back to bed. I have another present for you."

Makenna could see the desire she felt mirrored in Vanessa's eyes. "You have to make a pecan pie this morning, remember?"

Vanessa smiled. "We've got time. And then we'll call Declan."

Makenna narrowed her eyes and they crinkled as she began to smile. She didn't say a word as she got up, took Vanessa's hand and led them to the bedroom.

19

Makenna drove into her parents' driveway with the luscious aroma of a freshly baked pie invading her car.

"I think I'm going to have pie before I eat anything else. It smells so good it's making me woozy."

Vanessa laughed. "Are you sure something else isn't making you woozy?" She cut her eyes sideways and smirked.

"Do you mean my other Christmas present?"

"Maybe," Vanessa answered suggestively.

Makenna's cheeks reddened. "That may be the best Christmas present I've ever received."

"Maybe? You mean it wasn't the best?" Vanessa scoffed.

"Christmas isn't over yet," she said playfully.

"Oh, that's right."

"Do you think Santa has something else for me?"

"Well, you have been a very good girl lately," Vanessa said, wiggling her eyebrows.

Makenna threw her head back and laughed. "I love you," she said, reaching over and kissing Vanessa.

"I love you, too."

They opened the front door to a plethora of tantalizing smells, making them even hungrier. Vanessa's pecan pie added to the aromas.

"Merry Christmas!" Makenna called, walking inside then holding the door for Vanessa.

"There they are," Makenna's brother, Luke, said. "Hi Sis. And Vanessa. It is so nice to see you again."

"Thanks Luke, it's nice to see you, too." Vanessa remembered him as a nice guy always ready with a smile. "You look exactly the same."

"Well you don't," he stated.

Makenna and Vanessa looked at one another.

"You are even more beautiful. I told my wife that all the guys wanted to know who the new girl was that summer, but Makenna won your heart."

"She sure did," Vanessa said, gazing at Makenna.

"Can I take that pie for you?" A woman Vanessa assumed was Luke's wife walked up to them with a smile.

"Vanessa, this is my wife, Beth."

"Hi Beth. It's so nice to meet you. I've got it, let me take it to the kitchen."

Beth and Vanessa went to the kitchen while Luke and Makenna trailed behind them. Makenna couldn't help but feel grateful they had taken to Vanessa with such warmth. But she wasn't surprised because Vanessa had a way with people.

"This looks delicious," Luke said as Vanessa set the pie on the island with the other dishes.

"I've heard they are," Jean said, squeezing Vanessa's shoulders from behind. "Merry Christmas."

"Merry Christmas to you." Vanessa turned and smiled at Jean, but her eyes quickly searched for Makenna. She spotted her across the kitchen nodding as if to say, 'You're okay. I'm right here.' Vanessa shyly smiled back.

Makenna walked over to her mom. "Mom," she said quietly. "Look." She pointed to the necklace.

Her mom looked down and her eyes lit up. "From Vanessa?"

Makenna smiled and nodded, her eyes full of happiness.

"It's beautiful." She looked at Makenna and then Vanessa. "Would those be birthstones?"

"Yes," Vanessa answered.

"I'm going to guess that one is yours," she said, nodding at Vanessa. "And the other one is...Declan's?"

Makenna's eyes shone. Vanessa jumped in. "It was his idea. He can be a bit pushy when it comes to your daughter."

"I think it's lovely," Jean replied. "Well, what about yours?" she continued, raising her eyebrows then looking down at Vanessa's hand.

She quickly brought her hand up for Jean to see the ring. "Oh," she said, her head tilting. "It's beautiful. She tried to describe it to me over the phone." Jean looked at Makenna. "Very nice, sweetie."

"Thanks, Mom."

"Hi Aunt Makenna," Owen said, walking up and giving her a hug.

"Merry Christmas, O," she said fondly. "I'd like you to meet my girlfriend," she said without hesitating. "This is Vanessa."

"Hi, it's nice to meet you."

Before she could respond another boy came in and swooped Makenna into a hug. "Merry Christmas to my favorite aunt!"

After being bear hugged, Makenna laughed. "And this is Hank."

"Hi Vanessa. I've heard all about you."

"Dude!" Owen exclaimed.

Vanessa laughed. "It's nice to meet both of you. I've actually heard all about you, too. It seems you might know my son, Declan?" she said playfully.

Both boys' faces lit up. "We do. He is such a good vaulter," Hank said. "Owen's going to be that good in a couple of years."

"Hank!" Owen looked at Vanessa apologetically. "He gets excited. Hank is a runner, I'm the pole vaulter."

"I look forward to watching you both. I love track meets. I've gotten pretty good at them," she winked.

Makenna chuckled. "I guess you have been to quite a few."

"Never missed one of his meets yet and don't plan to. Moving here will make that a little easier."

"Hey everyone, let's open presents and then eat," Doug said from the living room.

"Hey Dad," Makenna said, giving him a hug.

"Hi Doug, we missed you when we came in," Vanessa said, hugging him as well.

"I was teaching my grandsons a thing or two about video games."

"Oh yeah?" Vanessa asked, surprised.

"He's pretty good. I wouldn't be surprised," Makenna said.

After the family gathered, Jean and Doug played Santa and passed out gifts.

"Wait, I thought you'd already opened gifts," Makenna said.

"We have," Luke said. "I have something for you and Vanessa. And I think Mom and Dad held back one for the boys."

"For us?" Vanessa asked.

"Yeah. Here," Luke said. "Actually it's from me and Beth."

Makenna nodded at Vanessa to open the rectangular package. She ripped the wrapping paper off to reveal a framed photograph.

Vanessa gasped, immediately recognizing the photo. She showed it to Makenna and turned to Luke. "Where did you get this?"

"I actually took it. Back then I dabbled in photography. Not long ago I came across some old rolls of film. Beth is a photographer and developed them. Most were out of focus landscapes and a few of friends, but then I saw this one and couldn't believe it."

"You never showed this to me," Makenna said, marveling at the photo. She and Vanessa were standing side by side, one arm hanging around the other's shoulder in their swimsuits at the pool where Makenna was a lifeguard. The smiles on their faces as they looked at the camera were full of youthful love and innocence.

"I didn't want to upset you," he said quietly.

"I remember you taking this picture," Vanessa said, staring at it. "Right after you took it, I shoved Makenna into the pool."

"I remember that now. Luke, you dared her, didn't you?"

"Yep. It was something like that." He looked at Vanessa. "When Makenna told me you were back in town, I had Beth enlarge it. I thought it would look great in your house." He immediately looked uncomfortable. "Uh, I mean, in one of your houses. Um..."

"It's okay." Vanessa laughed. "We're going to redo my grandparents' house." She and Makenna both admired the photo.

"Thank you both so much. This is the best gift," Makenna said. She looked over at Vanessa and said quietly, "I'll say it this time. It's a Christmas miracle."

Vanessa chuckled. "This one really is, don't you think?"

Makenna agreed, nodding her head fervently.

After the presents were opened everyone filled their plates. Jean had the dining room table set festively and they all gathered around to enjoy the food, laughter, and family.

Everyone pitched in to clean up the meal. Leftovers were distributed among the families. There was one piece of Vanessa's pecan pie left that she gave to Doug.

"Aunt Makenna, we get to come to the first track meet like we did last year, don't we?" asked Hank.

"Oh course you do. I'll have passes so we can get in the infield too."

"I can hardly wait," said Owen. "Hey, do you think if they're practicing on a Saturday I could come watch sometime?"

"I don't see why not. Let me check with the coach. I'll let you know."

"Thanks," Owen said, hugging her goodbye. "It was really nice to meet you, Vanessa."

"You too, Owen. I'm sure I'll be seeing you again soon."

Hank hugged Makenna next. "Thanks for the Christmas money. It's always the perfect size," he said, winking.

Makenna laughed, shaking her head. She loved Hank's sense of humor and Owen's big heart. Their schedules were full and she didn't get to see them enough, but FaceTime calls helped.

They hugged everyone else, promising to see them tomorrow, then left them for their Christmas naps.

"That was so much fun!" Vanessa said on the way home.

"It really was. Those boys! I just love them to pieces," Makenna said, laughing.

"I can see why. They are too much."

"Is it nap time for us, too?" Makenna asked.

Vanessa whipped her head around. "Are you tired? Do you want to nap?"

"Whoa, no. I was just asking."

"I thought we were going on a hike?"

"That's the plan, but we're changing clothes first, right?"

"Oh, yeah. That would be a good idea."

"Are you all right, babe? You're acting a little funny."

Vanessa sighed. "No, I'm fine. It's just—" She paused. "Your family is so nice to me. And that photo! Isn't it perfect for our house?" Before Makenna could answer she continued, "Did you see our faces? My mother didn't have to go through my stuff; you could see we were head over heels in love just by looking at us."

Makenna laughed and grabbed her hand. "And still are," she said, kissing the back of her hand.

"I can't wait to get to those trees," Vanessa murmured as she looked out the window.

"What?" Makenna asked, not sure she heard her right.

"I'm just glad we're going hiking. I've been looking forward to it," Vanessa said, trying to slow her beating heart down. She felt like she'd been waiting twenty-five years for this, yet Makenna didn't have a clue.

She pulled into the driveway and they went inside to change. Vanessa changed quickly then hurried to the living room and found what she was looking for in her bag. She was putting Makenna's surprise in her pocket when she heard her come down the hall.

"All ready?" Makenna asked, smiling.

"I'm ready," Vanessa said, taking a deep breath.

"Let's go."

20

M akenna drove into the parking lot and noticed there were a couple of cars already parked there. It looked like they weren't the only ones that needed exercise on this Christmas day.

They got out and Vanessa grabbed a small backpack that contained water as well as her phone. Makenna locked the car and they walked to the trailhead.

"Do you want me to take that?" Makenna asked.

"Nope, I've got it." Vanessa adjusted it on her back. "I do need your hand though," she said, reaching out to Makenna.

Makenna smiled and took her hand. She stopped and brought them up in front of her. "Would you look how well they fit together."

Vanessa stared and took a deep breath to calm her heart. "Come on," she said, taking a step and swinging their hands as they walked down the path. They walked side by side for a while enjoying the crisp air and movement for their bodies after the big meal.

"I can't tell you how much I love this. Do you think we could do it every week?" Vanessa asked as she stopped at a break in the trees to look down at the valley.

"Sure we could. Next time we can start by going past the love trees, as you call them, and continue around the loop that Declan ran that day, then end up back at the car."

"Okay, but we're stopping at our trees today, too."

"Our trees. I like that," Makenna said.

"Is this the way?" Vanessa asked, seeing the faint mark of a trail.

"That's it. Good job, babe. You've only been here once and you can already recognize the path."

"Maybe they're calling to me now, too."

Makenna smiled and walked behind her until they came to the small clearing, stopping when the tangled trees appeared right in front of them.

Vanessa took the backpack off and reached for her phone inside. She pulled up a playlist, turned up the volume and pushed play.

"What's this?" Makenna asked.

"Would you dance with me?" Vanessa reached out her hand.

Makenna gave her a confused look, but she took her hand. Vanessa placed her hands on Makenna's hips as Makenna wrapped her arms around Vanessa's neck. Makenna listened for a moment and then her face lit up with recognition.

"Oh my God. That's 'I Swear' by All 4 One. We listened to this every night that summer."

"We did," Vanessa whispered. She pulled Makenna close and sang the lyrics into her ear.

Makenna swooned in Vanessa's arms. "This is the most romantic thing ever," she murmured as Vanessa continued to sing softly.

Vanessa danced them over until they were right in front of the trees. They swayed until the song ended. She kissed the spot right below Makenna's ear and whispered, "I love you so."

Makenna tightened her arms and held Vanessa to her, burning this moment into her memory. "I love you, too."

Vanessa leaned her head back and looked into Makenna's eyes. Her heart was beating wildly and she was sure Makenna could feel it through their shirts, but when their eyes met she felt calm. Slowly she eased away and bent down on one knee.

Makenna's eyes grew wider than Vanessa had ever seen them and she threw her hands over her mouth in surprise.

Vanessa smiled and reached up for one of her hands. She clasped it in both of hers and kissed the back of Makenna's hand. Then she looked up into Makenna's eyes that glistened with tears. "I have finally found my way home. But home isn't a town or a house, Kenna. You are my home. Your heart is the only place I want to live. With you is the only place I can be myself completely. I love you with all I am, with all I have, with all I will be. Makenna Markus, will you marry me?"

"Yes, yes, yes!" Makenna exclaimed, pulling Vanessa up so she could kiss her.

"Wait!" Vanessa said before their lips could meet. She reached into her pocket and pulled out a diamond engagement ring. Her hand was shaky and her smile was huge as she slipped the ring onto Makenna's waiting finger.

Breathlessly Makenna said, "It's beautiful!" She continued to stare at the ring until Vanessa put her hands on either side of her face.

"Now we kiss," she said, nodding and giggling.

Makenna mirrored Vanessa's hands and looked from her eyes to her lips and back to her eyes. "I can't wait to marry you." The distance between their lips closed instantly.

What started as cold lips meeting on a wintry Christmas day turned into a heated, passionate kiss. As the heat rose their lips parted and their tongues met.

"Mmm," Vanessa moaned, dropping her hands to Makenna's hips and pulling her as close as she could get her. She felt promises and shared joy and so much love she thought her heart would explode. Their tongues danced and caressed and pledged never ending love to one another.

When their lips parted their foreheads pressed together. Makenna smiled and closed her eyes, letting the tears run free.

Vanessa ran her thumbs under both her eyes, wiping her tears. "I didn't mean to make you cry."

"I missed you, I yearned for you, I ached for you for so long. And now you're right here. You're right here in my arms. I don't want to ever let you go," Makenna said passionately.

"Then don't," Vanessa said simply.

Makenna nodded. "I won't."

Vanessa started the music again and they danced, wrapped around one another just like the love trees.

This was the best Christmas ever!

ONE YEAR LATER

"My moms always talk about this Christmas Stroll so I hope you like it, Amy," Declan said from the back seat.

"I'm sure I will." She leaned forward slightly and asked, "How long have you been coming here?"

Vanessa looked over at Makenna and grinned, her eyebrows raised. "Well, this will be our third time. The other two were quite far apart."

"Declan told me it was a long time ago, but I didn't quite understand."

Vanessa looked into the rearview mirror and met Declan's eyes for approval. He nodded. The last thing she wanted to do was embarrass him because Amy had become very important in his life. Makenna had remarked the other night that he looked at Amy the way Vanessa looked at her.

"Well, the first time we came here was twenty-six years ago," Vanessa began.

"He's told me about your love story and I'd really like to hear it from the both of you," Amy interrupted excitedly.

Vanessa exchanged a look with Makenna and began again. "I spent the summer here and then came back for Christmas twenty-six years ago. We'd fallen in love and I really wanted to walk down the street hand in hand with my girl here." She held her hand up so Makenna could take it.

"Your girl," she chuckled. "But she wouldn't do that in town because she was afraid it would get back to her parents somehow. So, we heard about this Christmas Stroll and came here."

"What happened?"

"We walked around town hand in hand and no one paid us any attention. It was wonderful," Vanessa said, squeezing Makenna's hand.

"It really was. So, when she came back last year we decided to drive over again. We found the neatest little shop and bought our first ornament together for our Christmas tree."

"Isn't that the same shop you got my snow globe in?"

"Same one."

"The one you keep on your desk? It looks like you!" Amy exclaimed.

"That's what I thought," Makenna explained. "Anyway, this is a special place for us and we're glad you two decided to join us this year."

"That's a nice story, but their wedding story is even better," said Declan.

"Oh? Would you share?"

Vanessa and Makenna laughed. "I don't know why you think that's so special. It was just one of your mom's Christmas miracles," Makenna said, giving Vanessa a sideways glance.

"I haven't heard of too many people proposing one day and getting married the next," replied Declan.

"Come on, you have to tell it now. You can't leave me hanging," Amy urged.

"Have you and Declan gone hiking in the park to the entwined trees?" Makenna asked.

"Yes, he told me they were your trees."

Vanessa chuckled. "They kind of are. Last Christmas Day we

hiked to them and I proposed." The smile on her face grew as the memories came back.

Makenna sighed. "That was so romantic." She turned in her seat slightly and looked at Amy. "She had a playlist of songs we listened to during the summer we fell in love and we danced around those trees."

Amy gasped. "How romantic!"

"You sang in my ear," Makenna said, running her hand along Vanessa's shoulder, studying her face as she watched the road.

"Do you remember the song?" Amy asked, obviously enthralled with the story.

"Of course I do, but you won't know it."

"I might, what was it?"

"'I Swear' by All 4 One."

Amy grabbed her phone and began searching for the song. In a few moments the music filtered through the car.

"That's it!" said Vanessa. "But I only sing it to my girl," she said, sneaking a look at Makenna and winking.

Makenna giggled and Declan said exasperatedly, "Oh my God."

Amy playfully slapped him on the shoulder. "Don't be like that. It's romantic. What happened next?"

"She bent down on one knee and proposed."

"Were you surprised?"

"A little. I'd been thinking about doing the same thing, but we hadn't talked about it."

"Now to the good part," said Declan.

Vanessa laughed. "When Kenna said yes, she meant right then."

"Not exactly. We danced for a bit and *we*," she said with emphasis, "We decided, why wait? If we could've gotten a license that day we would've done it right then."

"The next day we got the license. Makenna's brother happened to be in town and he'd gotten ordained for a wedding he did for a friend earlier that month. So he married us. Declan stood up for both of us and Makenna's parents and brother's family were there."

"But where did you have the ceremony?" Amy asked.

Vanessa and Makenna looked at one another and shrugged. "At the trees, of course," they said together.

"Oh wow! That is such a good story."

Vanessa drove into the parking lot and pulled into a space. "It was miracle after miracle," she said, looking at Makenna. "It was the best Christmas ever."

Makenna tilted her head. "So far."

"So far," Vanessa agreed.

They got out and walked around, looking at the shops. When they got to the shop with the ornaments they found another for their tree. They left Declan and Amy in the store and strolled down the sidewalk.

They walked along hand in hand just like always, bumping shoulders, stealing glances. The lights were twinkling, the smell of evergreens and cinnamon wafted through the air, and the Christmas music serenaded them as they came to the big trees in the square.

Vanessa pulled Makenna behind one and she gasped.

"I don't know why that surprises me, you do it every time we come here," she said, grinning. Her arms found their way around Vanessa's neck then she placed her hands on the back of Vanessa's shoulders, pulling them chest to chest.

"Is there anything better than walking down the street hand in hand with your girl?" Vanessa said breathlessly.

"Yes," Makenna said softly. "Marrying her." She brought their lips together in a soft sensual kiss filled with passion and love.

She pulled back slightly and with tears in her eyes she looked into Vanessa's. She saw them glisten with want, need, adoration, and love.

With a slight smile she whispered, "You will always be my Christmas miracle, Nessa."

Their lips met again in a kiss sprinkled with Christmas magic.

ABOUT THE AUTHOR

Jamey Moody is a small town Texas girl that loves romance. She lives with her little terrier Leo that brings her toys every time she walks in the house. If she's not reading or writing you can catch her on her bike, paddleboard, or in the middle of an adventure.

Jamey would love to hear from you! Contact her at jameymoodyauthor@gmail.com or at her website www.jameymoodyauthor.com

If you would be so kind and leave a review on Amazon or Goodreads, I'd be grateful!

Find her on social media.

Printed in Great Britain
by Amazon